THE TERRANS IN TROUBLE!

A crackle of static blared from the screen. A pale, alien visage with five stalked eyes stared out at Retief and Magnan.

"To identify yourselves at once, rash interlopers!" a weak voice hissed. "To be gone instanter or suffer dire consequences!"

"It's Broodmaster Slith, Retief!" cried Magnan.

"Withdraw at once or take responsibility for precipitation of a regrettable incident!" snarled Slith. "In sixty seconds I order my gunners to fire!"

Then a rasping, high-pitched voice cut in from the auxiliary screen. The image of a shiny, purplish-red cranium formed on the screen, knobbed and spiked, with eyes mounted on outriggers that projected a foot on either side.

"I outrage! I do not endure! You are gave one minutes, Eastern Standard Time, for total abandon of vicinity. *Counting! Nine, twelve, two, several—*"

Books by Keith Laumer

The Best of Keith Laumer
Fat Chance
The Glory Game
A Plague of Demons
Retief and the Warlords
Retief of the CDT
Retief's War

Published by TIMESCAPE/POCKET BOOKS

RETIEF OF THE CDT
Keith Laumer

A TIMESCAPE BOOK
PUBLISHED BY POCKET BOOKS NEW YORK

ACKNOWLEDGMENTS

All of the stories appearing in this volume were first published in *If*. "Mechanical Advantage," originally published as "Retief, Long Awaited Master," copyright © 1969 by Galaxy Publishing Corp. "Ballots and Bandits," copyright © 1970 by UPD Publishing Corp. "Pime Doesn't Cray," copyright © 1971 by UPD Publishing Corp. "Internal Affair," copyright © 1971 by UPD Publishing Corp. "The Piecemakers," copyright © 1970 by Universal Publishing & Distributing Corp.

A Timescape Book published by
POCKET BOOKS, a Simon & Schuster division of
GULF & WESTERN CORPORATION
1230 Avenue of the Americas, New York, N.Y. 10020

Published by arrangement with Doubleday & Company, Inc.
Library of Congress Catalog Card Number: 73-150902

ISBN: 0-671-43406-3

First Pocket Books printing July, 1978

10 9 8 7 6 5 4 3

POCKET and colophon are trademarks of Simon & Schuster.

Use of the TIMESCAPE trademark under exclusive license
from trademark owner.

Printed in the U.S.A.

FOR JOE AND GAY

Contents

RETIEF
OF THE CDT

Ballots and Bandits

Second Secretary Retief of the Terran Embassy emerged from his hotel into a bunting-draped street crowded with locals: bustling, furry folk with upraised, bushy tails, like oversized chipmunks, ranging in height from a foot to a yard. A party of placard-carrying marchers, emerging from a side street, jostled their way through the press, briskly ripping down political posters attached to shop walls and replacing them with posters of their own. Their move was immediately countered by a group of leaflet distributors who set about applying mustaches, beards, and crossed eyes to the new placards. The passers-by joined in cheerfully, some blacking out teeth and adding warts to the tips of button noses, others grabbing the brushes from the defacers and applying them to their former owners' faces. Fists flew; the clamor rose.

Retief felt a tug at his knee; a small Oberonian dressed in blue breeches and a spotted white apron looked up at him with wide, worried eyes.

"Prithee, fair sir," the small creature piped in a shrill voice, "come quick, ere all is lost!"

"What's the matter?" Retief inquired, noting the flour smudge on the Oberonian's cheek and the dab of pink icing on the tip of his nose. "Are the cookies burning?"

"E'en worse than that, milord—'tis the Tsuggs! The great brutes would dismantle the shop entire! But follow and observe!" The Oberonian whirled and darted away.

Retief followed along the steeply sloping cobbled alley between close-pressing houses, his head level with the second-story balconies. Through open windows he caught glimpses of dollhouselike interiors, complete with toy tables and chairs and postage-stamp-sized TV screens. The bright-eyed inhabitants clustered at their railings, twittering like sparrows as he passed. He picked his way with care among the pedestrains crowding the way: twelve-inch Ploots and eighteen-inch Grimbles in purple and red leathers, two-foot Choobs in fringed caps and aprons, lordly three-foot-six-inch Blufs, elegant in ruffles and curled pink wigs. Ahead, he heard shrill cries, a tinkle of breaking glass, a dull thump. Rounding a sharp turn, he came on the scene of action.

Before a shop with a sign bearing a crude painting of a salami, a crowd had gathered, ringing in a group of half a dozen giant Oberonians of a type new to Retief: swaggering dandies in soiled silks, with cruelly cropped tails, scimitars slung at their waists—if creatures of the approximate shape of tenpins can be said to have waists. One of the party held the bridles of their mounts—scaled, spike-maned brutes resembling gaily painted rhinoceri, but for their prominent canines and long, muscular legs. Two more of the oversized locals were busy with crowbars, levering at the lintel over the shop doorway. Another pair were

12

briskly attacking the adjacent wall with sledge hammers. The sixth, distinguished by a scarlet sash with a pistol thrust through it, stood with folded arms, smiling a sharp-toothed smile at the indignant mob.

" 'Tis the pastry and ale shop of Binkster Druzz, my granduncle twice removed!" Retief's diminutive guide shrilled. "A little light hearted destruction in the course of making one's political views clear is all very well—but these pirates would reduce us to penury! Gramercy, milord, canst not impede the brutes?" He swarmed ahead, clearing a path through the onlookers. The red-sashed one, noticing Retief's approach, unfolded his arms, letting one hand linger near the butt of the pistol—a Groaci copy of a two-hundred-year-old Concordiat sliver-gun, Retief noted.

"Close enough, Off-worlder," the Tsugg said in a somewhat squeaky baritone. "What would ye here? Yer hutch lieth in the next street yonder."

Retief smiled gently at the bearlike Oberonian, who loomed over the crowd, his eyes almost on a level with Retief's own, his bulk far greater. "I want to buy a jelly doughnut," the Terran said. "Your lads seem to be blocking the doorway."

"Aroint thee, Terry; seek refreshment elsewhere. Being somewhat fatigued with campaigning, I plan to honor this low dive with my custom; my bullies must needs enlarge the door to comport with my noble dimensions."

"That won't be convenient," Retief said smoothly. "When I want a jelly doughnut I want it now." He took a step toward the door; the pistol jumped at him. The other Tsuggs were gathering around, hefting crowbars.

"Ah-ah," Retief cautioned, raising a finger—and at the same moment swung his foot in a short arc that ended just under the gunhandler's knee joint. The victim emitted a sharp yap and leaned forward far enough for his jaw to intersect the course of Retief's left fist. Retief palmed the gun deftly as the Tsugg staggered backward into the arms of his companions.

"Aroint thee, lads," the giant muttered reproachfully to his supporters, shaking his head dazedly. "We've been boon drinking chums these six Lesser Moons, and this is the first time ye've give me any of the good stuff. . . ."

"Spread out, lads," one of the Tsuggs ordered his companions. "We'll pound this knave into a thin paste."

"Better relax, gentlemen," Retief suggested. "This gun is messy at short range."

"An' I mistake me not," one of the crowbar wielders said, eying Retief sourly, "ye're one of the Outworld bureaucrats, here to connive in the allocation of loot, now the Sticky-fingers have gone."

"Ambassador Clawhammer prefers to refer to his role as refereeing the elections," Retief corrected.

"Aye," the Tsugg nodded, "that's what I said. So how is it ye're interfering with the free democratic process by coshing Dir Blash in the midst of exercising his voice in local affairs?"

"We bureaucrats are a mild lot," Retief clarified, "unless someone gets between us and our jelly doughnuts."

Red-sash was weaving on his feet, shaking his head. " 'Tis a scurvy trick," he said blurrily, "sneaking a concealed anvil into a friendly little six-to-one crowbar affray."

"Let's go," one of the others said, "ere he produces a howitzer from his sleeve." The *banditti* mounted their wild-eyed steeds amid much snorting and tossing of fanged heads.

"But we'll not forget yer visage, Outworlder," another promised. "I wot well we'll meet again—and next time we'll be none so lenient."

A hubbub of pleased chatter broke out among the lesser Oberonians as the party passed from sight.

"Milord hast saved Greatuncle Binkster's fried fat this day," the small being who had enlisted Retief's aid cried. The Terran leaned over, hands on knees, which put his face on a level only a foot or two above that of the little fellow.

"Haven't I seen you before?" he asked.

"Certes, milord—until an hour since, I eked out a few coppers as third assistant pastrycook in the inn yonder, assigned to the cupcake division, decorative-icing branch." he sighed. "My specialty was rosebuds —but no need to burden Your Grace with my plaint."

"You lost your job?" Retief inquired.

"Aye, that did I—but forsooth, 'tis but a trifling circumstance, in light of what I o'erheard ere the hostler bade me hie me from the premises forthwith!"

"Let's see, your name is . . . ?"

"Prinkle, milord. Ipstitch Prinkle IX, at your service." The Twilpritt turned as a slightly plumper, grayer version of himself bustled up, bobbing his head and twitching his ears in a manner expressive of effusive gratitude. "And this, milord, is Uncle Binkster, in the flesh."

"Your sarvent, sir," Uncle Binkster squeaked, mopping at his face with a large striped handkerchief. "Wouldst honor me by accepting a cooling draft of pring-lizard milk and a lardy-tart after milord's exertions?"

"In sooth, Uncle, he needs something stronger than whey," Prinkle objected. "And in sooth, the Plump Sausage offers fine ale—if Your Grace can manage the approaches," he added, comparing Retief's six-foot-three with the doorway.

"I'll turn sideways," Retief reassured the Oberonian. He ducked through, was led across the crowded room by a bustling eighteen-inch tapman to a corner

15

table, where he was able to squeeze himself onto a narrow bench against the wall.

"What'll it be, gents?" the landlord inquired.

"Under the circumstances, I'll stick to small beer," Retief said.

"Ale for me," Uncle Binkster said. " 'Tis vice, perchance, to tipple ere lunchtime, but with Tsuggs roaming the Quarter battering down walls, one'd best tipple while opportunity presents itself."

"A sound principle," Retief agreed. "Who are these Tsuggs, Uncle Binkster?"

"Lawless rogues, down from the high crags for easy pickings," the elderly baker replied with a sign. "After you Terrans sent the Groaci packing, we thought all our troubles were over. Alas, I fear me 'tis not the case. So soon as the ruffians got the word the Five-eyes were pulling out, they came swarming down out of the hills like zing-bugs after a jam-wagon—'tis plain they mean to elect their ruffianly chief, Hoobrik the Uncouth. Bands of them roam the city, and the countryside as well, terrorizing the voters—" He broke off as the landlord placed a foaming three-inch tankard before Retief.

"Away with that thimble, Squirmkin!" he exclaimed. "Our guest requires a heartier bumper than that!"

" 'Tis an Emperor-sized mug," the landlord said, "but I allow his dimensions dwarf it. Mayhap I can knock the top out of a hogshead . . ." He hurried away.

"Pray, don't mistake me, milord," Uncle Binkster resumed. "Like any patriot, I rejoiced to see the Sticky-finger go, leaving the conduct of Oberonian affairs to Oberonians. But who'd have guessed we normal-sized chaps would at once be subjected to depredations by our own oversized kith and kin exceeding anything the invaders ever practiced!"

"A student of history might have predicted it," Re-

16

tief pointed out, "But I agree: Being pushed around by local hoodlums is even less satisfying than being exploited from afar."

"Indeed so," Prinkle agreed. "In the case of foreigners one can always gain a certain relief by hurling descriptive epithets, mocking their outlandish ways, and blaming everything on their inherent moral leprosy—an awkward technique to use on one's relatives."

The landlord returned, beaming, with a quart-sized wooden container topped by a respectable head. Retief raised it in salute and drank deep.

"And if what my nephew o'erheard be any indication," Uncle Binkster went on, wiping foam from his whiskers, "the worst is yet to come. Hast related all to our benefactor, lad?"

"Not yet, Uncle." Prinkle turned to Retief. "I was sweeping up crumbs in the VIP breakfast room, my mind on other matters, when I heard the word 'Tsugg' bandied among the company still sitting at table. I cocked an auricle, thinking to hear the scoundrels roundly denounced, only to catch the intelligence that their chief, that brawling bravo Hoobrik, representing himself to be spokesman and natural leader of all Obernon, withal, hath demanded audience of His Impressiveness, Ambassador Clawhammer! 'Twas but natural that I undertook to disabuse Their Lordships of this impertinent notion, accidentally overturning a pot of chocolate in process thereof—"

"Alas, my nephew is at times too enthusiastic in his espousal of his views," Uncle Binkster put in. "Though 'tis beyond dispute, in this instance he was sorely tried."

"In sooth, so was His Honor, Mr. Magnan, when the cocoa landed in his lap," Prinkle admitted. "Happily, 'twas somewhat cooled by long standing."

"A grotesque prospect," Uncle Binkster ruminated. "Those scapegrace villains lording it over us honest

17

folk! Perish the thought, Sir Retief! I trow I'd sooner have the Five-eyes back!"

"At least they maintained a degree of control over the ne'er-do-wells," Prinkle said, "restricting them to their hills and caves."

"As will we, lad, once the election is consummated," Uncle Binkster reminded the youth. "Naturally, we Twilpritts stand ready to assume the burden of policing the rabble, as is only right and natural, so soon as our slate is elected, by reason of our superior virtues—"

"Hark not to the old dodderer's maunderings, Giant," a tiny voice peeped from the next table. A miniature Oberonian, no more than nine inches tall, raised his one-ounce glass in salute. "We Chimberts, being Nature's noblemen, are of course divinely appointed to a position of primacy among these lumbering brutes, saving your presence, milord—"

"Dost hear a dust-cricket chirping in the woodwork?" a medium-sized Oberonian with black circles resembling spectacles around his eyes inquired loudly from three tables away. " 'Twere plain e'en to an Outworlder that we Choobs are the rightful inheritors of the mantle of superiority. Once in office we'll put an end to such public rantings."

"You in office?" Prinkle yelped. "O'er my dead corse, varlet!" He leaped up, slopping beer as he cocked his arm to peg the mug at the offender.

"Stay, Nephew!" Uncle Binkster restrained the youth. "Pay no heed to the wretch. Doubtless he's in his cups—"

"Drunk, am I, you old sot!" the Choob yelled, overturning the table as he leaped up, grabbing for the hilt of his foot-long sword. "I'll ha' a strip o' thy wrinkled hide for that allegation—" His threat was cut off abruptly as a tankard, hurled from across the room, clipped him over the ear, sending him reeling into the next table, whose occupants leaped up with indignant shouts and flailing fists.

"Gentlemen, time, time!" the landlord wailed, before diving behind the bar amid a barrage of pewter. Retief finished his beer in a long swallow, and rose, looming over the battle raging about his knees.

"A pleasure, gentlemen," he addressed the room at large. "I hate to leave such a friendly gathering, but Staff Meeting time is here."

"Farewell, Sir Retief," Prinkle panted from under the table, where he grappled with a pale-furred local of about his own weight. "Call around any time for a drop and a bit of freindly political chat."

"Thanks," Retief said. "If things get too slow in the frontline trenches I'll remember your invitation."

2

As Retief entered the conference room—a converted packing room in the former warehouse temporarily housing the Terran Mission to the newly liberated planet Oberon—First Secretary Magnan gave him a sour look.

"Well—here you are at last. I'd begun to fear you'd lingered to roister with low companions in your usual manner."

"Not quite my usual manner," Retief corrected. "We'd barely started to roister when I remembered Staff Meeting. By the way, what do you know about a fellow called Hoobrik the Uncouth?"

Magnan looked startled. "Why, that name is known only to a handful of us in the inner security circle," he said in a lowered tone, glancing about. "Who leaked it to you, Retief?"

"A few hundred irate locals. They didn't seem to know it was a secret."

"Well, whatever you do, act surprised when the Ambassador mentions it," Magnan cautioned his junior as they took seats at the long table. "My," he went on as the shouts of the crowd outside the building rose to a thunderous level, "how elated the locals are, now they realize we've relieved them of the burdens of Groaci overlordship! Hear their merry cries!"

"Remarkable," Retief agreed. "They have a better command of invective than the Groaci themselves."

"Why, Wilbur," Magnan said as Colonel Saddlesore, the Military Attaché, slipped into the chair beside him, avoiding his glance. "However did you get that alarming discoloration under your eye?"

"Quite simple, actually." The Colonel bit off his words like bullets. "I was struck by a thrown political slogan."

"Well!" Magnan sniffed. "There's no need for recourse to sarcasm."

"The slogan," Saddlesore amplified, "was inscribed on the rind of a bham-bham fruit of the approximate size and weight of a well-hit cricket ball."

"I saw three small riots myself on the way into the office," the Press Attaché said in a pleased tone. "Remarkable enthusiasm these locals show for universal suffrage."

"I think it's time, however," the Counselor put in ponderously, "that someone explained to them that the term 'political machine' does not necessarily refer to medium tank."

The chatter around the long table cut off abruptly as Ambassador Clawhammer, a small, pink-faced man with an impressive paunch, entered the room, glowered at his staff as they rose, waved them to their seats as he waited for silence.

"Well, gentlemen"—he looked around the table—

"what progress have you to report anent the preparation of the populace for the balloting?"

A profound silence ensued.

"What about you, Chester?" Clawhammer addressed the Counselor. "I seem to recall instructing you to initiate classes in parliamentary procedure among these riffraff—that is to say, among the free citizens of Oberon."

"I tried, Mr. Ambassador. I tried," Chester said sadly. "They didn't seem to *quite* grasp the idea. They chose up sides and staged a pitched battle for possession of the chair."

"Ah—I can report a teensy bit of progress in my campaign to put across the idea of one man, one vote," a slender-necked Political Officer spoke up. "They got the basic idea, all right . . ." He paused. "The only trouble was, they immediately deduced the corollary: One *less* man, one *less* vote." He sighed. "Luckily, they were evenly matched, so no actual votes were lost."

"You might point out the corollary to the corollary," Retief suggested: "The lighter the vote, the smaller the Post Office."

"What about your assigned task of voter registration, eh, Magnan?" the Chief of Mission barked. "Are you reporting failure too?"

"Why, no, indeed, sir, not exactly failure; at least not *utter* failure; it's too soon to announce *that*—"

"Oh?" The Ambassador looked ominous. "When do you think would be an appropriate time? *After* disaster strikes?"

"I'd like to propose a rule limiting the number of political parties to P minus 1, P being the number of voters," Magnan said hastily. "Otherwise we run the risk that no one gets a plurality."

"No good, Magnan," the Counselor for PR Affairs spoke up. "We don't want to risk a change of meddling. However," he added thoughtfully, "we might just up the nomination fee to a figure sufficiently astronomical to keep the trash out—that is, to discourage the weakly motivated."

"I don't know, Irving." The Econ Officer ran his fingers through his thinning hair in a gesture of frustration. "What we really need is to prune the ranks of the voters more drastically. Now, far be it from me to propose strong-arm methods—but what if we tried out a modified Grandfather Rule?"

"Say—a touch of the traditional *might* be in order at that, Oscar," the Political Officer agreed tentatively. "Just what did you have in mind?"

"Actually, I haven't worked out the details; but how about limiting the franchise to those who have grandfathers? Or possibly grandchildren? Or even both?"

"Gentlemen!" Ambassador Clawhammer cut short the debate. "We must open our sights! The election promises to degenerate into a debacle of ruinous proportions, career-wise, unless we break through with a truly fresh approach!" He paused impressively.

"Fortunately," he continued in the modest tones of Caesar accepting the crown, "I have evolved such an approach." He raised a hand in kindly remonstrance at the chorus of congratulations that broke out at his announcement.

"It's clear, gentlemen, that what is needed is the emergence of a political force which will weld toegther the strands of Oberonian political coloration into a unified party capable of seating handy majorities. A force conversant with the multitudinous benefits which would stem from a sympathetic attitude toward Terran interests in the Sector."

"Yes, Chief," an alert underling from the Admin Section took his cue. "But, gosh, who could possibly produce such a miracle from the welter of divergent political creeds here on Oberon, which they're at practically swords' points with each other over each and every question of policy, both foreign and domestic?"

Clawhammer nodded acknowledgment. "Your question is an acute one, Dimplick. Happily, the answer is at hand. I have made contact, through confidential channels, with a native leader of vast spiritual influence who bids fair to fulfill the role to perfection." He paused to allow the staff to voice spontaneous expressions of admiration, then raised a palm for silence.

"While 'Golly' and 'Wow!' are perhaps less elegant effusions than one might logically expect from an assemblage of senior career diplomats," he said sternly, but with a redeeming twinkle in his small, red-rimmed eyes, "I'll overlook the lapse this time on the basis of your obvious shock at receiving such glad tidings after your own abysmal failures to produce any discernible progress."

"Heavens, sir, may we know the name of this messiah?" Magnan chirped. "When do we get to meet him?"

"Curious that you should employ that particular term with reference to Hoobrik," Clawhammer said complacently. "At this moment, the guru is meditating in the mountains, surrounded by his chelas, or disciples, known as Tsuggs in the local patois."

"Did you say . . . Hoobrik?" Magnan queried uncertainly. "Goodness, what a coincidence that he should have the same name as that ruffian of a bandit chief who had the unmitigated effrontery to send one of his strong-arm men to threaten Your Excellency!"

Clawhammer's pink features deepened to a dull magenta which clashed sharply with his lime-green early-late-mid-afternoon hemi-demi-informal seersucker dickey-suit. "I fear, Magnan," he said in a tone like a tire iron striking flesh, "that you've absorbed a number of erroneous impressions. His Truculence, Spiritual Leader Hoobrik, dispatched an emissary, it's true, to

23

propose certain accommodations sphere-of-influence-wise; but to proceed from that circumstance to an inference that I have yielded to undue pressures is an unwarranted speculative leap!"

"Possibly I just misinterpreted his messenger's phraseology, sir," Magnan said with a tight little smile. "It didn't seem to me that 'foreign bloodsuckers' and 'craven paper-pushers' sounded all that friendly."

"IPBMs may fry our skins, but words will never hurt us,' eh, sir?" the Econ Officer piped brightly, netting himself a stab of the Ambassadorial eye.

"Still, it's rather strong language," Colonel Saddlesore spoke up to fill the conversational gap. "But I daresay you put the fellow in his place, eh, Mr. Ambassador?"

"Why, as to that, I've been pondering the precisely correct posture to adopt vis-à-vis the Tsuggs, protocolwise. I confess for a few moments I toyed with the idea of a beefed-up 804-B: Massive Dignity, with overtones of Leashed Ire; but cooler counsels soon prevailed."

"How about a 764, sir?" the Econ Officer essayed: "Amused Contempt, with just a hint of Unpleasant Surprises in the Offing?"

"Too subtle," Colonel Saddlesore grunted. "What about the old standby, 26-A?"

"Oh, the old 'Threat To Break Off Talks' ploy, eh, Wilbur? Embellished with a side issue of Table-shape Dispute, I assume?"

"Gentlemen!" Clawhammer called the conference to heel. "You forget that the date of the elections is rushing toward us! We've no time for traditional maneuvers. The problem is simple: how best to arrive at a meeting of the minds with the guru."

"Why not just call him in and offer to back him in a take-over, provided he plays ball?" the PR Chief proposed bluntly.

"I assume, Irving," Clawhammer said into the shocked silence, "that what you actually meant to suggest was that we give His Truculence assurances of Corps support in his efforts to promote Oberonian welfare, in the event of his securing the confidence of the electorate, as evinced by victory at the polls, of course."

"Yeah, something like that," Irving muttered, sliding down in his chair.

"Now," Clawhammer said, "the question remains, how best to tender my compliments to His Truculence, isolated as he is in his remote fastness . . ."

"Why, simple enough, sir," Magnan said. "We just send a messenger along with an invitation to tea. Something impressive in a gold-embossed, I'd suggest."

"I understand this fellow Hoobrik has ten thousand blood-thirsty cutthroats—ah, that is, wisdom-hungry students—at his beck and call," the Econ Officer contributed. "They say anybody who goes up there comes back with his tail cropped."

"Small hazard, since we Terries have no tails," Magnan sniffed.

"I've got a funny feeling they'd figure out something else to crop," Oscar retorted sharply.

"Am I to infer, Magnan, you're volunteering to convey the bid?" Clawhammer inquired blandly.

"Me, sir?" Magnan paled visibly. "Heavens, I'd love to—except that I'm under observation for possible fourth-degree coca burns."

"Fourth-degree burns?" Colonel Saddlesore wondered aloud. "I'd like to see that. I've heard of first, second, and third degree, but—"

"The symptoms are invisible to lay inspection," Magnan snapped. "Additionally, my asthma is aggravated by high altitudes."

"By gad," Colonel Saddlesore whispered to his

neighbor, *"I'd* like a chance to confront these fellows . . ."

"Better wear your armor, Wilbur," his confidant replied. "From all reports, they weigh in at three hundred pounds, and wear six-foot cutlasses, with which they lay about them freely when aroused. And they say the sight of a Terry arouses them worse than anything."

". . . but, as I was about to say, my duties require that I hole up in my office for the forseeable future," the Colonel finished.

"Cutlasses, you say?" the Econ Officer pricked up his ears. "Hmm. Might be a market here for a few zillion up-to-date hand weapons—for police use only, of course."

"Capital notion, Depew." The Political Officer nodded approvingly. "Nothing like a little firepower to bring out the natural peace-loving tendencies of the people."

"Now, gentlemen—let us avoid giving voice to any illiberal doctrines," Clawhammer said sharply. "Our only motive, let us remember, is to bring the liberated populace to terms with the political realities—in this case, the obvious need for a man on horseback—or should I say a Tsugg on Vorchback?" The Terran envoy smiled indulgently at his whimsy.

"I have a question, Mr. Ambassador," Retief said. "Since we're here to supervise free elections, why don't we let the Oberonians work out their own political realities?"

Clawhammer looked blank.

"Just-ah-how do you mean?" the Political Officer prompted uneasily.

"Why don't we let them nominate whoever they want, and vote for any candidate they like?" Retief explained.

"I suggest you forget these radical notions, young

26

fellow," Clawhammer said sternly. "These free elections will be conducted in the way that free elections have always been conducted. And now that I've considered the matter, it occurs to me it might be valuable experience for you to pay the proposed call on His Truculence. It might serve to polish your grasp of protocol a trifle."

"But, sir," Magnan spoke up. "I need Mr. Retief to help me do the Consolidated Report of Deliquent Reports Reports—"

"You'll have to manage alone, I fear, Magnan. And now, back to the ramparts of democracy, gentlemen! As for you Retief . . ." The Ambassador fixed the latter with a poniard-sharp eye: "I suggest you comport yourself with a becoming modesty among the Tsuggs. I should dislike to have a report of any unfortunate incident."

"I'll do my best to see that no such report reaches you, sir," Retief said cheerfully.

3

The green morning sun of Oberon shone down warmly as Retief, mounted on a wiry Struke, a slightly smaller and more docile cousin of the fierce Vorch tamed by the Tsuggs, rode forth from the city gates. Pink and yellow borms warbled in the treetops; the elusive sprinch darted from grass tuft to grass tuft. The rhythmic whistling of doody-bugs crying to their young supplied a somnolent backdrop to the idyl.

Retief passed through a region of small, tidy farms, where sturdy Doob peasants gaped from the furrows. The forest closed in as the path wound upward into the foothills. In midafternoon he tethered the Struke and lunched beside a waterfall on paté sandwiches and sparkling Bacchus Black from a cold flask. He was just finishing off his *mousse éclair* when a two-foot-long steel arrow whistled past his ear to bury itself six inches in the dense blue wood of a nunu tree behind him.

Retief rose casually, yawned, stretched, took out a vanilla dope stick and puffed it alight, at the same time scanning the underbrush. There was a quick movement behind a clump of foon bushes; a second bolt leaped past him, almost grazing his shoulder, to rattle away in the brush. Appearing to notice nothing, Retief took a leisurely step toward the nunu tree, slipped suddenly behind it. With a swift motion, he grasped a small, limber branch growing out at waist height on his side of the two-foot bole, bent it down and pegged the tip to the shaggy, porous bark, using the match-sized dope stick to pin it in place. Then he moved quickly off, keeping the tree between himself and the unseen archer, to the concealment of a dense patch of shrubbery.

A minute passed; a twig popped. A bulky, tattooed Tsugg appeared, a vast, dumpy figure clad in dirty silks, holding a short, thick, recurved bow clamped in one boulderlike fist, a quarrel nocked, the string drawn. The dacoit tiptoed forward, jumped suddenly around the tree. Finding his quarry fled, he turned, stood with his back to the tree peering into the undergrowth.

At that moment, the bent branch, released by the burning of the dope stick, sprang outward, ramming the astounded bowman in the seat of his baggy green velveteen trousers. The arrow smacked into the dirt at his feet as he jumped, then stood rigid.

"Don't strike, sir!" he urged in a plaintive tenor. " 'Twas the older lads put me up to it . . ."

Retief strolled forth from shelter, nodded easily to the Tsugg, plucked the bow from his nerveless grip.

28

"Nice workmanship," he said, inspecting the weapon. "Groaci trade goods?"

"Trade goods?" the Tsugg said with a note of indignation. "Just because yer partner has a dirk at me back's no cause to make mockery of me. I plundered it from the Five-eyes all open and aboveboard, so help me."

"Sorry," Retief said. He withdrew the arrow from the loam, fitted it to the bow experimentally.

"You're not by chance a member of Hoobrik's band, are you?" he inquired off-handedly.

"Too right it's not by chance," the Tsugg said emphatically. "I went through the Ordeal, same's the other lads."

"Lucky we met," Retief said. "I'm on my way to pay a call on His Truculence. Can you lead me to him?"

The Tsugg straightened his 290 pound bulk. "Tell yer crony to do his worst," he said with a small break in his voice. "Fim Gloob's not the Tsugg to play the treacher."

"It wasn't exactly treachery I had in mind," Retief demurred. "Just ordinary diplomacy."

"Yer threats will avail ye naught," Fim Gloob declared.

"I see what you mean," Retief said. "Still, there should be some way of working this out."

"No outsider goes to the camp of Hoobrik but as a prisoner." The Tsugg rolled his shiny black eyes at the Terran. "Ah, sir—would ye mind asking yer side-kick not to poke so hard? I fear me he'll rip me weskit, stole for me by me aged mums it were, a rare keepsake."

"Prisoner, eh, Fim? By the way, I don't have a side-kick."

"That being the way of it," Fim Gloob said carefully, after a short, thoughtful pause, "who'd be the villain holding the blade to me kip glands?"

29

"As far as I know," Retief said candidly, "there's nobody here but you and me."

The Tsugg turned his head cautiously, peered behind him. With a grunt of annoyance, he snapped a finger at the offending bough.

"Me and me overactive imagination," he snorted. "And now," he went on, turning to Retief with a scowl—

"Remember, I still have the bow," Retief said pleasantly.

"And a mort o' good it'll do ye," Fim snarled, advancing. "Only a Tsugg born and bred has the arm to draw that stave!"

"Oh?" Retief set the arrow and with an easy motion pulled until the arrowhead rested against the bow, the latter being bent into a sharp curve. Another inch—and the stout laminated wood snapped with a sharp *twang!*

"I see what you mean," Retief said. "But then the Groaci always did produce flimsy merchandise."

"You . . . you broke it!" Fim Gloob said in tones of deep dismay.

"Never mind—I'll steal you a new one. We have some ladies' models in the Recreation Kits that ought not to overstrain you."

"But—I'm reckoned the stoutest bowman in the band!"

"Don't give it another thought, Fim. They'll love you when you bring in a live Terry, singlehanded."

"Who, me?"

"Of course. After all, I'm alone and unarmed. How could I resist?"

"Aye—but still—"

"Taking me in as a prisoner would look a lot better than having me saunter in on my own and tell Hoobrik you showed me the route."

"Wouldst do such a dirty trick?" Fim gasped.

"I wouldst—unless we start immediately," Retief assured the Tsugg.

"O.K." Fim sighed. "I guess I know when I'm licked. I mean when *you're* licked. Let's go, prisoner. And let's hope His Truculence is in a good mood. Otherwise, he'll clap ye on the rack and have the whole tale out of ye in a trice!"

4

A few dozen heavyweights lazing about the communal cooking pot or sprawling in the shade under the striped awnings stretched between the trees looked up in mild interest as Retief appeared on Strukeback, Fim Gloob behind him astride his Vorch, glowering ferociously as he verbally prodded the lone Terran forward.

"Ho, that's far enough, varlet!" he roared. "Dismount, whilst I seek instruction o' His Truculence whether to h'ist ye out of hand, or ha' a bit o' sport wi' ye first!"

"Ha, what be this, Gloob?" a bulky outlaw boomed as Retief swung down from the saddle. "An Off-worlder, I trow!"

" 'Tis no Oberonian, 'tis plain," another offered. "Mayhap 'tis a two-eyed variety o' Five-eyes."

"Avaunt ye, rogues!" Fim yelled. "Clear the way! I've fetched this Terry here to divert the great Hoobrik wi' his saucy sayings!"

"Saucy sayings, is it! I've had enough o' yer own saucy sayings, "Gloob! Methinks I'll split the creature on the spot!" The speaker drew a giant cutlass with a whistle of honed metal.

"Stay, Zub Larf!" a mountainous Tsugg in soiled

yellow robes bellowed. " 'Tis but dull, idling here in camp. I say let's see a sample o' the oddling's tricks, ere we slit his weasand."

"Here, what passes?" a familiar baritone cut through the clamor. A large Tsugg in a red sash pushed through the mob, which gave way grudgingly, with much muttering. The newcomer halted with a jerk when his eye fell on Retief.

"Methinks," he said, "I've seen you before, sirrah."

"We've met," Retief acknowledged.

"Though all you Terries look alike to me . . ." Dir Blash fingered his jaw gingerly. "Meseemeth 'twas in the Street of the Sweetmakers . . ."

"So it was."

"Aha! I've got it!" Dir Blash clapped Retief on the shoulder. "My boon companion! Ah, bullies," he addressed his fellows, "this Terry gave me a shot of something with a kick like a Vorch—though for the life of me I can't recall the precise circumstances. How wert thou yclept again, sirrah?"

"Retief. Lucky you have the kind of memory you do, Dir Blash; your compatriots were just debating the best method of putting me out of my misery."

"Say you so?" Dir Blash looked around threateningly, his hand on the hilt of his cutlass. "Nobody murders my drinking buddies but me, wot thee well, my hearties!" He turned back to Retief.

"Say, you wouldn't chance to have any more of the same, would you?"

"I'm saving it for a special occasion," Retief said.

"Well, what could be more special than a reprieve from being staved out on a zing-wasp hive, eh?"

"We'll celebrate later," Retief said. "Right now I'd appreciate a short interview with His Truculence."

"If I use my influence to get you in, wilt let me have another sample later?"

"If things work out as they ususally do," Retief said, "I think you can be sure of it."

"Then come along, Dir Retief. I'll see what I can do."

5

Hoobrik the Uncouth, lounging in a hammock under a varicolored canopy, gazed indifferently at Retief as Dir Blash made the introductions. He was an immense Tsugg, above the average height of his kind, his obesity draped in voluminous beaded robes. He selected a large green berry from a dented silver bowl at his elbow, shook exotic salts over it from a heavy gold saltshaker, and popped it into his mouth.

"So?" he grunted, spitting the seeds over the side. "Why disturb my meditations with trifles? Dispose of the creature in any way that amuses you, Blash-but save the head. I'll impale it on a pike and give it to the Terry chieftain—gift-wrapped, of course."

Dir Blash nodded, scratching himself under the ribs. "Well, thus doth the tart disintegrate, Retief," he said in tones of mild regret. "Let's go—"

"I don't want to be a spoilsport, Your Truculence," Retief spoke up, "but Ambassador Clawhammer only allows his staff to be decapitated at Tuesday morning Staff Meetings."

"Staff Meetings?" Hoobrik wondered aloud. "Is that anything like a barbecue?"

"Close," Retief agreed. "Quite often a diplomat or two are flayed alive and roasted over a slow fire."

"Hmm." Hoobrik looked thoughtful. "Mayhap I should introduce the custom here. 'Tis my wish to keep up with the latest trends in government."

"In that connection," Retief said, offering the stiff

parchment envelope containing the invitation to the reception, "His Excellency the Terrestrial Ambassador Extraordinary and Minister Plenipotentiary presents his compliments, and requests me to hand you this."

"Eh? What be this?" Hoobrik fingered the document gingerly.

"Ambassador Clawhammer requests the honor of your company at a ceremonial affair celebrating the election," Retief explained.

"Ceremonial affair?" Hoobrik shifted uneasily, causing the hammock to sway dangerously. "What kind of ceremony?"

"Just a small semiformal gathering of kindred souls. It gives everyone a chance to show off their clothes and exchange veiled insults face to face."

"Waugh! What kind of contest is this? Give me a good hand-to-hand disemboweling contest any day!"

"That comes later," Retief said. "It's known as Dropping by the Residence for a Drink After the Party."

"It hath an ominous sound," Hoobrik muttered. "Is it possible you Terries are more ferocious than I'd suspected?"

"Ha!" Dir Blash put in. "I myself dispatched half a dozen of the Off-worlders but this morn, when they sought to impede my entrance to a grog shop in the village."

"So?" Hoobrik yawned. "Too bad. For a moment, things were beginning to look interesting." He tore a corner off the gold-edged invitation and used it to poke at a bit of fruit rind wedged between his teeth. "Well, off with you, Blash—unless you want to play a featured role at my first Staff Meeting."

"Come, Terry," the red-sashed Tsugg growled, reaching for Retief's arm. "I just remembered the part of yesterday's carouse that had slipped my mind."

"I think," Retief said, evading the subchief's grab,

34

"it's time for that jolt I promised you." He stepped in close and rammed a pair of pile-driver punches to Dir Blash's midriff, laced a hard right to the jaw as the giant doubled over and fell past him, out cold.

"Here!" Hoobrik yelled. "Is that any way to repay my hospitality?" He stared down at his fallen henchman. "Dir Blash, get up, thou malingerer, and avenge my honor!"

Dir Blash groaned; one foot twitched; he settled back with a snore.

"My apologies, Your Truculence," Retief said, easing the Groaci pistol from inside his shirt. "Protocol has never been my strong suit. Having committed a *faux pas,* I'd best be on my way. Which route would be least likely to result in the demise of any of Your Truculence's alert sentries?"

"Stay, Outworlder! Wouldst spread tidings of this unflattering event abroad, to the detriment of my polling strength?"

"Word might leak out," Retief conceded. "Especially if any of your troops get in my way."

" 'Tis a shame not to be borne!" Hoobrik said hoarsely. "All Obernon knoweth that only a Tsugg can smite another Tsugg senseless." He looked thoughtful. "Still, if the molehill will not come to Meyer, Meyer must to the molehill, as the saying goeth. Since thou hast in sooth felled my liegeman, it follows you must be raised at once to Tsugghood, legitimizing the event after the fact, as it were."

"I'd be honored, Your Truculence," Retief said amiably. "Provided, of course, Your Truculence authorizes me to convey your gracious acceptance of His Exellency's invitation."

Hoobrik looked glum. "Well—we can always loot the Embassy afterward. Very well, Terry-Tsugg-to-be, that is. Done!" The chieftain heaved his bulk from the hammock, stirred Dir Blash with a booted toe, at which the latter groaned and sat up.

"Up, sluggard!" Hoobrik roared. "Summon a few varlets to robe me for a formal occasion! And my guest will require suitable robes, too." He glanced at Retief. "But don't don them yet, lest they be torn and muddied."

"The ceremony sounds rather strenuous," Retief commented.

"Not the Ceremony," Hoobrik corrected. "That commeth later. First cometh the Ordeal. If you survive that, I'll have my tailor fit you out as befits a subchief of the Tsugg!"

6

The Ceremonial Site for Ordeal Number One—a clearing on a forested slope with a breathtaking view of the valley below—was crowded with Tsugg tribesmen, good-naturedly quarreling, shouting taunts, offering and accepting wagers and challenges, passing wineskins from hand to grimy hand.

"All right, everybody out of the Ring of the First Trail," Dir Blash shouted, implementing his suggestion with hearty buffets left and right. "Unless ye plan to share the novitiate's hazards."

The mountaineers gave ground, leaving an open space some fifty feet in diameter, to the center of which Retief was led.

"All right, the least ye can do is give the Outlander breathing space." Dir Blash exhorted the bystanders to edge back another yard. "Now, Retief—this is a sore trial, 'tis true, but 'twill show you the mettle of us Tsuggs, that we impose so arduous a criterion on oursel's!" He broke off at a sound of crashing in the underbrush. A pair of tribesmen on the outer fringe of the audience flew into the air as if blown up by a mine, as with ferocious snorts, a wild Vorch, seven feet at the shoulder and armed with downcurving tusks, charged from the underbrush. His rush carried him through the ranks of the spectators, to burst into the inner circle, his short tail whipping, his head tossing as he sought a new target. His inflamed eye fell on Dir Blash.

"Botheration," the latter commented in mild annoyance as the beast lowered its head and charged. Leaning aside, the Tsugg raised a fist of the size and weight of a hand ax, brought it down with a resounding *bronggl* on the carnivore's skull. The unlucky beast folded in mid-leap, skidded chin-first to fetch up against Retief's feet.

"Nice timing," he remarked.

"Ye'd think the brute did it a-purpose, to pestificate a serious occasion," Dir Blash said disapprovingly. "Drag the silly creature away," he directed a pair of Tsuggs. "He'll be broke to harness for his pains. And now," he turned to Retief, "if ye're ready . . . ?"

Retief smiled encouragingly.

"Right, then. The first trial is: Take a deep breath, and hold it for the count of ten!" Dir Blash watched Retief's expression alertly for signs of dismay. Seeing none, he raised a finger disappointedly.

"Very well: Inhale!"

Retief inhaled.

"Onetwothreefourfivesixseveneightnineten," Dir Blash said in a rush, and stared curiously at the Terran, who stood relaxed before him. A few approving shouts rang out, then scattered handclaps.

"Well," Dir Blash grunted. "You did pretty fair, I

37

suppose, for an Outworlder. Hardly turned blue at all. You pass, I suppose."

"Hey," someone called from the front rank of the gallery. "He's not . . . ?"

"Not still . . . ?" someone else queried.

"Still holding his breath?" a third Tsugg said wonderingly.

"O' course not, lackwits!" Dir Blash bellowed. "How could he? E'en Grand Master Cutthroat Dirdir Hooch held out but to the count of twelve!" He looked closely at Retief. "Thou hast indeed resumed respiration . . . ?" He murmured.

"Of course," Retief reassured the Tsugg. "I was just grand-standing."

Dir Blash grunted. "In sooth, I've a feeling ye went a good thirteen, if truth were known," he muttered confidentially. "Hast made a specialty of suffocation?"

"Staff Meetings, remember?" Retief prompted.

"To be sure." Dir Blash looked disgruntled. "Well, on to the Second Trial, Terry. Ye'll find this one e'en a straiter test of Tsugghood than the last!" He led the way upslope, Retief close behind, the crowd following. The path deteriorated into a rocky gully winding up between near-vertical walls of rock. Pebbles rattled around the party from the crumbling cliffs above as members of the party clambered toward choice vantage points. A medium-sized boulder came bounding down from a crag to whistle overhead and crash thunderously away among the trees below. The journey ended in a small natural amphitheater, the floor of which was thickly littered with stones of all sizes. The spectators took up positions around the periphery above, as pebbles continued to clatter down around the tester and testee, who stood alone at the center of the target. A head-sized rock smashed down a yard from Retief. A chunk the size of a grand piano poised directly above him gave an ominous rumble and slid downward six inches amid a shower of gravel.

"What happens if one of those scores a bull's eye on the candidate?" Retief inquired.

"It's considered a bad omen," Dir Blash said. "Drat the pesky motes!" he added as a small fragment bounded off the back of his neck. "These annoyances detract from the solemnity of the occasion!"

"On the contrary," Retief demurred politely. "I think they add a lot of interest to the situation."

"Umm. Mayhap." Dir Blash gazed absently upward, moving his head slightly to avoid being brained by a baseball-sized missile. "Now, Outworlder!" he addressed Retief, "prepare for the moment of truth! Bend over"—he paused impressively—"and touch your toes!"

"Do I get to bend my knees?" Retief temporized.

"Bend whatever you like," Dir Blash said with airy contempt. "I trow this is one feat ye've not practiced at your Ordeal of the Staff Meeting!"

"True," Retief conceded. "The closest we come is lifting ourselves by our bootstraps." He assumed a serious expression, bent over, and with a smooth motion, touched his fingertips to his toes.

"Zounds!" someone called. "He did it in one try!"

"Didn't even take a bounce!" another added. Then the applause was general.

"Lacking in style," Dir Blash grumbled. "But a pass, I allow. But now you face the Third Ordeal, where yer tricks will do ye no good. Come along." As they moved off, his words were drowned as the stone piano crunched down on the spot he and Retief had just vacated.

The route to the Third Site led upward through a narrow cut to emerge on a bare rock slope. Fifty feet away a flat-topped rock spire loomed up from the depths, joined to the main mass of the peak by a meandering ribbon of rock some six inches in width, except where it narrowed to a knife edge, halfway across. Dir Blash sauntered out across the narrow bridge, gazing around him at the scenery.

"A splendid prospect, eh, Retief?" he called over his shoulder. "Look on it well; it may be thy last. What comes next has broken many a strong Tsugg down into a babbling Glert."

Retief tried the footing; it held. Keeping his eyes on the platform ahead, he walked quickly across.

"Now," Dir Blash said, "you may wish to take a moment to commune with your patron devils or whatever it is you Outlanders burn incense to, ere the Third Ordeal lays ye low!"

"Thanks, I'm in good shape incantationwise," Retief reassured his inquisitor. "Only last night I joined in a toast to the auditors."

"In that case . . ." Dir Blash pointed impressively to a flat stone that lay across two square rocks, the top of which cleared the ground by a good twelve inches.

"Leap the obstacle!" the subchief commanded. "In a single bound, mind you!"

Retief studied the hurdle from several angles before taking up his position before it.

"I see you hesitate," Dir Blash taunted. "Dost doubt thy powers at last, Terry?"

"Last year an associate of mine jumped fifty names

on the promotion list," Retief said. "Can I do less?" Standing flat-footed, he hopped over the barrier. Turning, he hopped back again.

There was a moment of stunned silence. Then pandemonium broke out. Dir Blash hesitated only a moment, then joined in the glad cries.

"Congratulations, Dir Tief!" he bellowed, pounding the Terran on the shoulder. "I warrant an Outworlder of thy abilities would be an embarrassment to all hands, but in sooth thou'rt now a Tsugg of the Tsuggs, and thy attainments are an adornment to our ilk!"

8

"Remarkable," said Hoobrik the Uncouth as he stuffed a handful of sugar-coated green olives into his mouth. "According to Blash here, you went through the Ordeal like a Tsugg to the pavilion born! I may keep you on as bodyguard, Dir Tief, after I get the vote out and myself in."

"Coming from Your Truculence, that's praise indeed." Retief said. "Considering your willingness to offer yourself as a candidate without a whimper."

"What's to whimper?" Hoobrik demanded. "After my lads have rounded up more voters than the opposition can muster, I'll be free to fill my pockets as best I may. 'Tis a prospect I face calmly."

"True," Retief said. "But first there are a few rituals to be gotten past. There's Whistle-stopping, Baby-kissing, Fence-sitting, and Mud-slinging, plus a considerable amount of Viewing-with-Alarm."

"Hmm." Hoobrik rubbed his chin thoughtfully. "Are these Ordeals the equal of our Rites of Tsugg-hood, Retief?"

"Possibly even worse," Retief solemnly assured the chieftain. "Especially if you wear an Indian war bonnet."

"Out upon it!" Hoobrik pounded his tankard on the table. "A Tsugg fears neither man nor beast!"

"But did you ever face a quorum of Women Voters?" Retief countered quickly.

"Nay—but my stout lads will ride down all opposition," Hoobrik declared with finality. "I've already made secret arrangements with certain Five-eyed Offworlders to supply me with all the write-in ballots I need to make everything legal and proper. Once in office, I can settle down to businesslike looting in an orderly manner."

"But remember," Retief cautioned, "you'll be expected to stand on your Party Platform—at least for the first few weeks."

"W-weeks?" Hoobrik faltered. "What is this platform, Retief?"

"It's a pretty shaky structure," Retief confided. "I've never known one to last past the first Legislative Rebuff."

"What, yet another Ordeal?"

"Don't worry about it, Your Truculence; it seldom goes as far as Impeachment."

"Well? Well? Don't keep me in suspense!" Hoobrik roared. "What doth this rite entail?"

"This is where your rival politicians get even with you for winning, by charging you with High Crimes and Misdemeanors—"

"Stay!" Hoobrik yelled. "Is there no end to these torments?"

"Certainly," Retief reassured the aroused leader. "After you retire, you become a Statesman, and are allowed out on alternate All Fools' Days to be queried as to your views on any subject sufficiently trivial to grace the pages of the Sunday Supplements."

"Arrrhh!" Hoobrik growled, and drained his mug. "See here, Retief," he said. "On pondering the matter, methinks 'twould be a gracious gesture on my part to take second place on the ticket and let a younger Tsugg assume party leadership; you, for example, Blash," he addressed the subchief.

"Who, me?" the latter blurted. "Nay, my liege—as I've said before, I am not now and do not intend to be a candidate!"

"Who, then?" Hoobrik waved his arms in agitation. "We need a Tsugg who'll appeal to a broad spectrum of voters! A good scimitarman, for beating down opposition inside the party, a handy club-wielder to bring in the Independents, a cool hand with a dirk, for committee infighting . . ." He paused, looking suddenly thoughtful.

"Well, I'll leave you gentlemen to look over the lists," Retief said, rising. "May I tell the Ambassador to expect you at the post-election victory reception?"

"We'll be there," Hoobrik said. "And I think I have a sure-fire Tsugg standard-bearer in mind to pull in the vote . . ."

9

In the varicolored glow of the lights strung in the hedges ringing the former miniature golf course pressed into service as Embassy grounds, the Terran diplomats stood in conversation clumps across the fairways and greens, glasses in hand, nervously eying the door through which Ambassador Clawhammer's entrance was expected momentarily.

"Gracious, Retief," Magnan said, glancing at his

watch, "the first results will be in any moment; I'm all a-twitter."

"I think we need have no fear of the outcome," Saddlesore stated. "Guru Hoobrik's students have been particularly active in these final hours, zealously applying posters to the polling places."

"And applying knots to the heads of reluctant converts," the Political Officer added. "What I'm wondering is—after Hoobrik's inauguration, what's to prevent his applying the same techniques to foreign diplomats?"

"Tradition, my boy," the Colonel said soothingly. "We may be shot as spies or deported as undesirable aliens; but shaped up by ward heelers, no."

There was a stir across the lawn; Ambassador Clawhammer appeared, ornate in the Burgundy cutaway and puce jodhpurs specified by CDT Regs for early evening ceremonial wear.

"Well? No word yet?" he stared challengingly at his underlings, accepting one of the four drinks simultaneously thrust at him by alert junior officers. "My private polls indicate an early lead for the Tsugg party, increasing to a commanding majority as the rural counties report."

"Commanding is right," Magnan muttered behind his hand. "One of the ruffians had the audacity to order me to hold his gluepot while he affixed a poster to the front door of the Embassy."

"What cheek," the Political Officer gasped. "You didn't do it?"

"Of course not," Magnan replied haughtily. *"He* held the gluepot, and *I* affixed the placard."

Happy shouts sounded from the direction of the gate; a party of Tsuggs appeared, flamboyant in pink and yellow, handing out foot-long yellow cigars. A throng of lesser Oberonians followed, all apparently in good spirits.

" 'Tis a landslide victory," one called to the assembly at large. "Break out the wassail bowl!"

"Is this official, Depew?" the Ambassador demanded of his Counselor, who arrived at that moment at a trot, waving a sheaf of papers.

"I'm afraid so—that is, I'm delighted to confirm the people's choice," he panted. "It's amazing; the Tsugg candidate polled an absolute majority, even in the oppositions' strongholds! It looks like every voter on the rolls voted the straight Tsugg ticket!"

"Certes, Terry," a Grimble confirmed jovially, grabbing two glasses from a passing tray. "We know a compromise candidate when we see one!"

" 'Tis a clear mandate from the people," a Tsugg declaimed. "Hoobrik will be along in a trice to help with sorting out the spoils. As for myself, I'm not greedy; a minor Cabinet post will do nicely."

"Out upon thee!" a jovial voice boomed as the Tsugg chieftain swept through the gate flanked by an honor guard of grinning scimitar-bearers. "No undignified rooting at the trough, lads! There's plenty to go around!"

"Congratulations, Your Truculence," Ambassador Clawhammer cried, advancing with outstretched hand. "I'm sure that at this moment you're feeling both proud and humble as you point with pride—"

"Humble!" Hoobrik roared. "That's for losers, Terry!"

"To be sure," Clawhammer conceded the point. "Now, Your Truculence, I don't want to delay the victory celebration, but why don't we just sign this little Treaty of Eternal Peace and Friendship set up to run for five years with a renewal option—"

"You'll have to speak to the new Planetary President about that, Terry." The chieftain waved the proffered document away. "As for myself, I have some important drinking to catch up on!"

"But I was informed by a usually reliable source" —Clawhammer turned to glare at the Counselor— "that the Tsugg party had carried off all honors!"

"True enough! By the way, where is he?"

"Where is who?"

"Our new Chief Executive, of course—" Hoobrik broke off, pushed past Clawhammer, rushed forward with outstretched arms, narrowly missing a small water hazard, to embrace Retief, who had just appeared on the scene.

"Stand aside, Retief," Clawhammer snapped. "I'm in the midst of a delicate negotiation—"

" 'Twere meet you employ a more respectful tone, Terry," Hoobrik admonished the Ambassador sternly. "Considering whom you're speaking to!"

"Who . . . whom I'm speaking to?" Clawhammer said in bewilderment. "Whom *am* I speaking to?"

"Meet Planetary President Dir Tief," Hoobrik said proudly, waving a hand at Retief. "The winner, and new champion!"

10

"Good lord, Retief." Magnan was the first to recover his speech. "When . . . ? How . . . ?"

"What's the meaning of this?" Clawhammer burst out. "Am I being made sport of?"

"Apparently not, Mr. Ambassador," Retief said. "It seems they put me on the ballot as a dark horse—"

"You'll be a horse of a darker color before I'm through with you!" Clawhammer yelled—and went rigid as twin scimitars flashed, ended with their points pressed against his neck.

"Bu-but how can a Terran be elected as head of the Tsugg party?" the Political Officer quavered.

"President Tief is no Terry, wittold!" Hoobrik corrected. "He's a Tsugg after my own heart!"

"But—doesn't the President have to be a natural-born citizen?"

"Art suggesting our President is *un*natural-born?" Hoobrik grated.

"Why, no—"

" 'Tis well. In that case, best you present your credentials at once, and we can get down to business."

As Clawhammer hesitated, a prod of the blade at his jugular assisted him in finding his tongue.

"Why, ah, Mr. President," he babbled, "er, I have the honor, et cetera, and will Your Excellency kindly tell Your Excellency's thugs to put those horrible-looking knives away?" His voice rose to a whispered shriek on the last words.

"Certainly, Mr. Ambassador," Retief said easily. "Just as soon as we've cleared up a few points in the treaty. I think it would be a good idea if the new Planetary Government has a solemn CDT guarantee of noninterference in elections from now on . . ."

"Retief—you wouldn't dare—" At a sharp nudge, Clawhammer yipped. "I mean, of course, my boy, whatever you say."

"Also, it would be a good idea to strike out those paragraphs dealing with CDT military advisers, technical experts, and fifty-credit-a-day economists. We Oberonians would prefer to work out our own fates."

"Yes—yes—of course, Mr. President! And now—"

"And as to the matter of the one-sided trade agreement: Why don't we just scrap that whole section and substitute a free-commerce clause?"

"Why—if I agree to that, they'll have my scalp, back in the Department!" Clawhammer choked.

"That's better than having it tied to a pole outside my tent," Hoobrik pointed out succinctly.

"On the other hand," Retief said, "I think we Tsuggs can see our way clear to supply a modest security force to ensure that nothing violent happens to the foreign diplomats among us as long as they stick to diplomacy, and leave all ordinary crime to us Oberonians."

"Agreed!" Clawhammer squeaked. "Where's the pen?"

It took a quarter of an hour to delete the offending paragraphs, substitute new wording, and affix signatures to the imposing document establishing formal relations between the *Corps Diplomatique Terrestrienne* and the Republic of Oberon. When the last length of red tape had been affixed and the last blob of sealing wax applied, Retief called for attention.

"Now that Terran-Oberonian relations are off on a sound footing," he said, "I feel it's only appropriate that I step down, leaving the field clear for a new election. Accordingly, gentlemen, I hereby resign the office of President in favor of my Vice-president, Hoobrik."

Amid the clamor that broke out, Clawhammer made his way to confront Retief.

"You blundered at last, sir!" he hissed in a voice aquiver with rage. "You should have clung to your spurious position long enough to have gotten a head-start for the Galactic periphery! I'll see you thrown into a dungeon so deep that your food will have to be lowered to you in pressurized containers! I'll—"

"You'll be on hand to dedicate the statue to our first Ex-President, I ween?" President Hoobrik addressed the Terran envoy. "I think a hundred-foot monument will be appropriate to express the esteem in which we hold our Tsugg emeritus, Dir Tief, eh?"

"Why, ah—"

"We'll appreciate your accrediting him as permanent Political Adviser to Oberon," Hoobrik continued. "We'll need him handy to pose."

"To be sure," Clawhammer gulped.

"Now I think it's time we betook ourselves off to more private surroundings, Dir Tief," the President said. "We need to plot party strategy for the coming by-election!"

"You're all invited to sample the hospitality of the Plump Sausage," Binkster Druzz spoke up. "Provided I have thy promise there'll be no breeching of walls."

"Done!" Hoobrik cried heartily. "And by the way, Dir Druzz, what wouldst think of the idea of a coalition, eh?"

"Hmm. . . . Twilprit sagacity linked with Tsugg bulk might indeed present a formidable ticket," Binkster concurred.

"Well, Retief," Magnan said as the party streamed toward the gate, "yours was surely the shortest administration in the annals of representational government. Tell me, confidentially: How in the world did you induce that band of thugs to accept you as their nominee?"

"I'm afraid that will have to remain a secret for now," Retief said. "But just wait until I write my memoirs."

Mechanical Advantage

"Twenty thousand years ago," said Cultural Attaché Pennyfool, "this, unless I miss my guess, was the capital city of a thriving alien culture."

The half-dozen Terrans—members of a Field Expeditionary Group of the *Corps Diplomatique Terrestrienne*—stood in the center of a narrow strip of turquoise-colored sward that wound between weathered slabs of porous, orange masonry, rusting spires of twisted metal to which a few bits of colored tile still clung, and anonymous mounds in which wildflowers nodded alien petals under the light of a swollen orange sun.

"Imagine," Consul Magnan said in an awed tone, as the party strolled on through a crumbling arcade and across a sand-drifted square. "At a time when we were still living in caves, these creatures had already developed automats and traffic jams." He sighed. "And now they're utterly extinct. The survey's life detectors didn't so much as quiver."

"They seem to have progressed from neon to nuclear annihilation in record time," Second Secretary Retief commented. "But I think we have a good chance of bettering their track record."

"Think of it, gentlemen," Pennyfool called, pausing at the base of a capless pylon and rubbing his hands together with a sound like a cicada grooming its wing cases. "An entire city in pristine condition—nay, more, a whole continent, a complete planet! It's an archaeologist's dream come true! Picture the treasures to be found: the stone axes and telly sets, the implements of bone and plastic, the artifacts of home, school, and office, the tin cans, the beer bottles, the bones—oh, my, the bones, gentlemen! Emerging into the light of day after all these centuries to tell us their tales of the life and demise of a culture!"

"If they've been dead for twenty thousand years, what's the point in digging around in their garbage dumps?" an Assistant Military Attaché inquired *sotto voce*. "I say Corps funds would be better spent running a little nose-to-ground reconnaissance of Boge, or keeping an eye on the Groaci."

"Tsk, Major," Magnan said. "Such comments merely serve to reinforce the popular stereotype of the crassness of the military mind."

"What's so crass about keeping abreast of the opposition?" the officer protested. "It might be a nice change if we hit them first, for once, instead of getting clobbered on the ground."

"Sir"—Magnan tugged at the iridium-braided lapels of his liver-colored informal field coverall—"would you fly in the face of six hundred years of tradition?"

"Now, gentlemen," Pennyfool was saying, "we're not here to carry out a full-scale dig, of course, merely to conduct a preliminary survey. But I see no reason why we shouldn't wet a line, so to speak.

51

Magnan, suppose you just take one of these spades and we'll poke about a bit. But carefully, mind you. We wouldn't want to damage an irreplaceable art treasure."

"Heavens, I'd love to," Magnan said as his superior offered him the shovel. "What perfectly vile luck that I happen to have a rare joint condition known as motorman's arm—"

"A diplomat who can't bend his elbow?" the other replied briskly. "Nonsense." He thrust the implement at Magnan.

"Outrageous," the latter muttered as his superior moved out of earshot, scanning the area for a likely spot to commence. "I thought I was volunteering for a relaxing junket, not being dragooned to serve as a navvy."

"Your experience in digging through Central Files should serve you in good stead, sir," Second Secretary Retief said. "Let's just pretend we're after evidence of a political prediction that didn't pan out by someone just above you on the promotion list."

"I resent the implication that I would stoop to such tactics," Magnan said loftily. "In any case, only an idiot would go on record with guesswork." He eyed Retief obliquely. "I, ah, don't suppose you know of any such idiot?"

"I did," Retief said. "But he just made Ambassador."

"Aha!" Pennyfool caroled from a heavy silted doorway flanked by a pair of glassless openings. "A well-nigh intact structure, quite possibly a museum. Suppose we just take a peek." The diplomats trailed their enthusiastic leader as he scrambled through into a roofless chamber with an uneven, dirt-drifted floor and bare walls from which the plaster had long since disappeared. Along one side of the room a flat-topped ridge projected a foot above the ground. Pennyfool poked a finger at a small mound atop it, exposing a lumpy object.

"Eureka!" he cried, brushing dirt away from his find. "You see, gentlemen? I've already turned up a masterpiece of the Late Meretricious!"

"I say, sir," a plump Third Secretary addressed the expedition's leader, "since Verdigris is a virgin world, and we're the first beings to set foot here since its discovery, how does it happen the era already has a name?"

"Simple, my boy," Pennyfool snapped. "I just named it."

"Look here, sir," an eager Information Agency man who had been poking at the find said, "I think there's been an error. This place isn't a museum; it's a lunch counter. And the masterpiece is a plate of petrified mashed potatoes and mummified peas."

"By Jove, I think you've got something there, Quagmire," a portly Admin Officer said. "Looks just like the stuff they served at the Testimonial Dinner for Ambassador Clawhammer—"

"He's right," Magnan announced from his position farther down the line. "Here's a side order of French fries—"

"Dunderheads!" Pennyfool snapped. "I'm not in need of uninformed conjectures by amateurs in order to properly classify priceless antiquities. Kindly leave such matters to experts. Now, come along. There seems to be an adjoining room with an intact roof—a room unvisited for twenty centuries! I'll wager my figleaf cluster to my *Grand Cordon* of the *Légion d'Cosme* that a thrilling discovery awaits us there!" His staff followed him past the edge of a metal door standing half open, into a dark chamber. The next moment, pale yellowish light flooded the room.

"To stop where you are," a weak voice hissed the words in a breathy alien tongue from behind the delegation. "To raise your digital members above your cephalic nodules, or to be incinerated on the spot!"

2

A spindle-legged creature in a flaring helmet and sequinned greaves emerged from the deep shadow of the door, aiming a scatter-gun carelessly at Magnan's knees.

"What's this?" Pennyfool's voice cracked on the words. "Groaci? Here?"

"Indeed, Soft One," the alien confirmed. "To comply at once with my instructions or to add your osseous components to those already interred here!"

Other gun-toting creatures appeared from alcoves and behind columns, closed in, clacking horny mandibles threateningly.

"See here, Captain," Pennyfool said in a high, nervous voice to a larger than average Groaci in jeweled eyeshields who carried no weapon but an ornamental side arm. "What's the meaning of this unwarranted interference with a peaceful party of duly authorized official personnel of the Corps Diplomatique Terrestrienne?"

"The meaning, Mr. Pennyfool," the officer replied in accent-free Terran, "is that you are anticipated, forestalled, preceded." He casually waved a dope stick in a foot-long ivory holder. "You are interlopers, trespassers on Groacian real estate; you note that out of delicacy I refrain from use of the term 'invaders.'"

"Invaders? We're scientists—art lovers—and—"

"To be sure," the captain cut him off curtly. "However, it will be necessary for you to indulge these fancies elsewhere. Verdigris, as an unoccupied planet, has been claimed by my government. Unfortunately, we are at present unable to issue tourist visas to the curious. You will therefore repair at once to your vessel, pay the accumulated landing fees, demurrage, fines for illegal parking, and lift tax, and be on your way—"

"This is an outrage, you five-eyed bandit!" the Assistant Military Attaché yelled, thrusting to the fore. "This planet was discovered by a Corps scouting vessel! It belongs to us!"

"I shall overlook your tone, Major," the Groaci whispered acidly, "induced no doubt by envy at my race's superior optical endowments, and simply inquire whether any Terran claim to the world was ever registered with the appropriate tribunals?"

"Of course not," Pennyfool snapped. "We didn't want every claim-jumping Tom, Dick, and Irving in this end of the Arm swarming in here to see what they could loot!"

"An unfortunate oversight, Mr. Pennyfool—"

"But the Survey boat planted a claim beacon. You must have seen it—"

"Dear me, now that you mention it, I seem to recall my chaps vaporizing some sort of electronic noise-maker which was interfering with radio reception. Too bad that not a trace remains."

"That's a gross violation of Interplanetory Rules!"

"So? Possession is nine points of the law, Mr. Pennyfool. But enough of these pleasantries; at the moment, the matter of accounts receivable requires our attention. I'm sure you're eager to clear up the trifling indebtedness and be about your no doubt legitimate activities elsewhere."

"How . . . how much," Pennyfool asked, "is this going to cost us?"

"If one of you will hand over twenty-two thousand

six hundred and four galactic credits, cash, no checks, please, you can be on your way."

"Twenty-two thousand!" Pennyfool choked on the words. "That's highway robbery!"

"Plus an additional thousand penalty fee for each insult," the captain added in an ominous whisper. "And of course I need not remind you that the demurrage charges are piling up minute by minute."

"That's out of the question," Pennyfool gasped. "I have no such amount in my possession! We're a scientific expedition, not a party of bank messengers!"

"Too bad," the captain whispered. "In that case . . ." He made a curt gesture; armed troops stepped forward, guns at the ready.

"Stop!" Magnan yelped. "You can't just shoot diplomats down in cold blood!"

"Since higher organisms such as myself employ no vascular fluids, I am under no such restraint," the captain pointed out. "However, I agree it would be less than couth to fail to observe the forms. Accordingly, I shall refer the matter to my chief." He murmured a word to a soldier, who slung his weapon and hurried away. The captain sauntered off, humming a gay little tune to himself.

"Verdigris was supposed to be the best-kept secret of the year," Pennyfool muttered brokenly to Magnan. "Who would have dreamed the Groaci would be here ahead of us. . . ?"

"They couldn't have found it by accident," the Information Agency man said glumly. "Coincidences like that don't happen."

"You're right, Crouchwell," Pennyfool said, staring around at his staff. "Gentlemen—somebody leaked!"

"Well, gracious, don't look at me, sir," Magnan said, an indignant expression pinching his narrow features. "*I* hardly breathed a word, except to a few highly respected colleagues."

"Colleagues?" Pennyfool raised a pale eyebrow.

"Fellow diplomats; high-type chaps like Ambassador P'Yim-Yim of Yill, and Slunk, the Fustian Minister, and . . . and . . ."

"And?" Pennyfool prompted.

"And Consul General Shilth," Magnan finished weakly.

"Planetary Director Shilth, if you don't mind," an alien voice spoke behind him. There was a stir among the troops ringing in the Terrans. A tall Groaci in an elaborately ribbed hip-cloak strolled forward, waved jauntily at Magnan, nodded to Pennyfool.

"Well, gentlemen, good of you to pay a courtesy call," he said smoothly.

"Mr. Consul General," Magnan said in a hurt tone. "I never dreamed you'd be so uncouth as to betray a confidence."

Shilth frowned, an expression he achieved by crossing two pairs of eyes. "No?" he said in a surprised tone. "Why not?" He vibrated his throat sac in a manner analogous to throat-clearing. "By the way, Pennyfool, just what was it you expected to find here?" His whisper was elaborately casual.

"You're standing in the center of a treasure house," Pennyfool said sourly, "and you have the confounded gall to ask me that?"

"My chaps have devoted the better part of the past ten hours to fruitless scrabbling in these ruins," Shilth hissed. "They've turned up nothing of the remotest utility."

"You've allowed your troops to dig here at random?" Pennyfool yelped.

"Aha!" Shilth wagged an accusatory tentacle. "In spite of your subtle dissembling, your reaction proves that treasures do indeed lie beneath this wilderness." His tone became crisp. "Kindly specify precisely what it is we're looking for, and I might—*might,* mind you —find a way to reduce your port fees."

"You . . . you assassin!" Pennyfool yelled. "You have no right to so much as set foot on this hallowed ground!"

"Still—I am here," Shilth said blandly. "And I see nothing in these rubble heaps to excite CDT interest." He stirred a heap of potsherds, bottle caps, and broken phonograph records with a horny foot. "Ergo, there must be a subtler prize awaiting the lucky finder."

"Shilth, you Vandal!" Pennyfool yelped. "Have you no reverence for anything?"

"Try me with gold," the Groaci said succinctly.

"You're out of your mind, you Philistine! I've told you I don't have any cash on hand!"

"You refuse to speak?" Shilth turned to the captain. "Thish, I tire of the Soft One's lies and his insults. Take him out and execute him." Pennyfool squealed as the guards laid hold of him.

"Execute him?" Magnan bleated. "Couldn't you just strike him off the invitation list for cocktail parties or something?"

"If it's gold you're interested in," Retief suggested, "I'm sure CDT Sector HQ will come through with a tidy sum in return for Mr. Pennyfool's hide, unbroken."

"Splendid notion," a member from the Commercial Section piped up. "I'm sure the ransom money—that is to say, the port fees—will be forthcoming the minute they see us all back at Sector HQ, safe and sound."

"Indeed?" Shilth said in a bored tone. "And if I allowed you to depart, what surety would I then have that the just indemnities will be paid?"

"You have the word of a diplomat," Magnan said promptly.

"I admire your coolness, Magnan," Shilth said with a little bow, "assaying jests at such a moment."

"I suppose I might consent to go alone," Pennyfool said, blinking his eyes rapidly. "Although of course I'd prefer to stay on as hostage myself, my rank will undoubtedly be helpful in expediting payment."

"One may go," Shilth said in a chilling whisper. *"That* one." He pointed at Retief. Thish stepped forward, pointing his overdecorated handgun at the victim.

"Watch him closely, Captain," Shilth admonished. "He has a reputation as a trouble-maker; as well have him off our hands—"

As Thish, close beside Retief, waved the gun toward the entrance, Retief, with a swift motion, swept the weapon from the other's grip, took a step, caught Shilth by the neck, and backed him against the wall, the muzzle of the pistol pressed against the hostage's ventral carapace.

"Tell your boys to stand fast," he said in a conversational tone as the Groaci official writhed and kicked futilely while the soldiers looked on as if paralyzed. "Mr. Pennyfool, if you're ready to board ship, I don't think Planetary Director Shilth will voice any objection."

"My soldiers will shoot you down like nesting nidfowls!" Shilth hissed.

"In which case, I'd be forced to pump your thorax full of soft-nosed slugs," Retief said. "I've heard they penetrate the exo-skeleton and then just ricochet around inside until they lose momentum. Be interesting to find out if it's true."

"I remind you, Pennyfool—" Shilth cocked his oculars at the Terran, who had not moved—"my lads' scatter-guns are highly disruptive to flimsy organisms such as yourselves. Disarm your misguided colleague, and spare the CDT the expense of a mass funeral, no less costly for lack of any identifiable remains!"

"Better get moving, sir, before some bright lad gets ideas," Retief suggested.

"They . . . we . . . I. . . ," Pennyfool gasped.

"By no means," Retief said soothingly. "They hold Shilth in far too high esteem to see him converted into a boiled pudding on the half shell."

Cautiously, the Terrans sidled toward the door. Pennyfool went through in a scrambling leap, followed closely by his associates.

"Retief," Magnan, at the rear of the party, said, "how are you going to get clear? If one of them gets behind you—"

"Better get aboard, Mr. Magnan," Retief cut in. "I have an idea Mr. Pennyfool won't dawdle around waiting for stragglers."

"But—but—"

"Captain Thish, perhaps you'd be kind enough to act as escort," Retief said, "just in case any of the boys on the outside leap to conclusions."

"To comply," Shilth whispered in Groaci as the officer hesitated. "Later, to visit this miscreant's crimes upon him in a fashion devised at leisure—*our* leisure, that is."

Magnan made a gobbling sound and disappeared, Thish at his heels. Shilth had stopped struggling. The Groaci soldiery stood in attitudes of alert paralysis, watching for an opening. It was ten minutes before the sound of the Corps vessel's drive rumbled briefly, faded, and was gone.

"And now?" Shilth inquired. "If you contemplate a contest of endurance, I remind you that we Groaci can carry on for upwards of ten standard days without so much as nictating a membrane."

"Send them outside," Retief said.

Shilth remonstrated, but complied. A moment later, a shrill but unmistakably human yelp sounded from beyond the door. Magnan appeared in the entry, his arms gripped by a pair of Groaci while a third held a scatter-gun to his head.

"They . . . they didn't wait," the diplomat wailed.

"Release me!" Shilth hissed. "Or would you prefer to wait until after my lads have blown your superior's head off?"

"Sounds like an even trade," Retief said. Magnan gasped and swallowed.

"Much as I should dislike to see the Planetary Director's internal arrangements hashed in the manner you so vividly described," Thish said from behind Magnan, "I assure you I would make the sacrifice in the interest of the Groaci national honor."

"In the interest of his next promotion, he means," Shilth hissed. "What does he care if I'm diced in the process?"

Retief thrust Shilth away, tossed the gun on the floor. "If I didn't know you wanted both of us alive, I'd have called your bluff, Thish," he said.

"Oh? And do I want you alive, Soft One?" Thish took aim with a borrowed rifle—

"Of course you do, littermate of genetic inferiors!" Shilth snapped, massaging the point on his back where the gun muzzle had dug in. "At least until they divulge the secret of what they sought here!" He turned to Retief. "And now let us to business, eh?"

Retief plucked a cigar from his breast pocket, puffed it alight, blew scented smoke past the alien's olfactory orifices, which cinched up tight at the aroma of Virginia leaf.

"Certainly, Shilth. Who's for sale now?"

"You are, my dear Terry," the Groaci said ominously. "The price of your life is a complete description of the nature and location of the riches hidden here."

Retief waved the stogie at the blotched walls, the

61

dirtdrifted corners, the broken tilework. "You're looking at them."

"Ah, so we are to have the pleasure of assisting you in developing a more cooperative attitude, eh? Capital. Easy babblers are such bores."

"You wouldn't dare torture us," Magnan said in squeaky tone. "Our colleagues know where we are. If we aren't returned unharmed, they'll extract a terrible vengeance!"

"A sharp note to the Ambassador, no doubt," Shilth said, with an amused snap of the mandibles. "Still, there are subtler methods of persuasion than living dismemberment. Now, we Groaci are quite at home in enclosed spaces; but you Terries, it is rumored, are claustrophobes, an allegation I've often yearned to test. And I know just the setting in which to conduct the experiment." He gestured to Thish, who urged the two Terrans at gunpoint along a wide passage to a metal door. Two soldiers came forward to wrestle the heavy panel aside, exposing a tiny chamber no more than six feet on a side, windowless, unfurnished.

"Gentlemen, your cell. A trifle cramped, perhaps, but well protected from excessive wind and rain, eh?"

Retief and Magnan stepped inside. The two soldiers forced the heavy sliding door shut.

In the total darkness, a dim spot of light glowed on one wall. Retief reached out and pressed a thumb against it.

With a grinding of ancient gears, a groaning of antique cables, the elevator started down.

3

Magnan emitted a shrill cry and attempted to climb the wall. "Retief! What's happening?"

"No, no, Mr. Magnan," Retief said. "Your line is, 'Ah, just as I planned.' That's the way reputations for forethought are built."

"Shilth was quite right about the claustrophobia," Magnan said in a choked voice. "I feel that the walls are going to close in on me!"

"Just close your eyes and pretend you're at a Tuesday morning Staff Meeting. The relief when you find yourself here should carry you through anything short of utter catastrophe."

"With a shudder and a clank, the car came to a halt.

"N-now what?" Magnan said in a small voice. Retief felt over the door, found the stub of a lever. He gripped it and pulled. Reluctantly, the door slid aside on a large, column-filled room faintly lit by strips of dimly glowing material still adhering to ceiling and walls, adorned with murals depicting grotesque figures engaged in obscure rites.

"Tomb paintings," Magnan said in a hushed voice. "We're in the catacombs. The place is probably full of bones, not that I actually believe in the curses of dead Kings or anything."

"The curses of live Ambassadors are far more potent, I suspect," Retief said, leading the way across the room and into one of the many passages debouching from the chamber. Here more cabalistic scenes were etched in still-bright colors against the ancient walls. Cryptic legends in an unknown script were blazoned across many of them.

"They're probably quotations from the local version of the Book of the Dead," Magnan hazarded, his eye caught by a vividly pigmented representation of a large alien being making what seemed to be a threatening gesture at a second alien from whose ears wisps of mist coiled.

"This one, for example," he said, "no doubt shows

us the God of the Underworld judging a soul and finding it wanting."

"Either that, or it's a NO SMOKING sign," Retief agreed.

The passage turned, branched. The left branch deadended at an ominous-looking sump half-filled with a glistening black fluid.

"The sacrificial well," Magnon said with a shudder. "I daresay the bottom—goodness knows how far down *that* is—is covered with the remains of youths and maidens offered to the gods."

Retief sniffed. "It smells like drained crankcase oil."

They skirted the pit, came into a wide room crowded with massive, complex shapes of corroded metal, ranked in rows in the deep gloom.

"And these are the alien idols," Magnan whispered. "Gad, they have a look of the most frightful ferocity about them . . ."

"That one"—Retief indicated a tall, many-armed monster-looming before him—"bears a remarkable resemblance to a hay-baler."

"Mind your tongue, Retief!" Magnan said sharply. "It's not that I imagine they can hear us, of course, but why tempt fate?"

There was a sharp *click!*, a whirring and clattering, a stir of massive forms all across the gloomy chamber. Magnan yipped and leaped back as a construct the size of a forklift stirred into motion, turned, creaking, and surveyed him with a pair of what were indisputably glowing amber eyes.

"We're surrounded," Magnan chirped faintly. "And they told us the planet was uninhabited!"

"It is," Retief said, as more giant shapes moved forward, accompanied by the squeak of unlubricated metal.

"Then what are these?" Magnan came back sharply. "Oversized spooks?"

"Close, but no kewpie doll," Retief said. "This is the city garage, and these are maintenance robots."

"R-r-robots?"

"Our coming in must have triggered them to come to alert status." They moved along the row of giant machines, each equipped with a variety of limbs, organs, and sensors.

"Then . . . then they're probably waiting for us to give them orders," Magnan said with returning confidence. "Retief! Don't you see what this means? We can tell them to jump in the lift and ride up and scare the nether garments off that sticky little Shilth and his army —or we could have done," he added, "if they understood Terran."

"Terran Understood," a scratchy bass voice rasped from a point just opposite Magnan's ear. He leaped and whirled, banging a shin smartly.

"Retief! They understand us! We're saved! Good lord, when I first planned our escape via the lift, I never dreamed we'd have such a stroke of luck!"

"Now you're getting the idea," Retief said admiringly. "But why not just add that extra touch of *savoir-faire* by pretending you'd deduced the whole thing, robots and all, from a cryptic squiggle on the contact party's scopegram?"

"Don't be crude, Retief," Magnan said loftily. "I fully intend to share the credit for the coup. In my report I'll mention that you pushed the lift button with no more than a hint from me."

"Maybe you'd better not write up that report just yet," Retief said, as a robot directly before them shifted position with a dry squeal of rusty bearing to squarely block their advance. Others closed in on either side; they turned to find retreat similarly cut off.

"My, see how eager they are, Retief," Magnan said in a comfortable tone. "There, there, just stand aside like a good, er, fellow." —

The machine failed to move. Frowning, Magnan started around it, was cut off by a smaller automaton —this one no bigger than a commercial sausage grinder, and adorned with a similar set of blades visible inside a gaping metallic maw.

"Well! I see they're in need of reprograming," Magnan said sharply. "It's all very well to fawn a little, but—"

"I'm not sure they're fawning," Retief said.

"Then—what in the world *are* they doing?"

"Terran are surrounded," a voice like broken glass stated from behind the encircled diplomats.

"We are judging Terran," an unoiled tenor stated from the rear rank, "and finding you wanting."

"Frightful oversized robots will jump on your smoking remains," chimed in a third voice, reminiscent of a file on steel.

"We are eager for crude contact," Broken Glass agreed.

"They have a curious mode of expressing themselves," Magnan said nervously. "I seem to detect an almost ominous note in their singular choice of words."

"I think they're picking up their vocabulary from us," Retief said.

"Retief—if it wasn't so silly, I'd think *that* one intended us bodily harm," Magnan said in a tone of forced jocularity, as a ponderous assemblage of sharp edges came forward, rumbling.

"We intend you bodily harm," File-on-steel said, advancing from the left.

"But—but you can't attack *us*," Magnan protested. "You're just machines! We're alive! We're your rightful masters!"

"Masters are better than robots," Broken Glass stated. "You are not better than us. You are not masters. We will certainly harm you."

"You will not escape," a red-eyed monster added.

"Retief—I suspect we've made a blunder," Magnan said in a wavering tone. "We were better off at the tender mercies of the Groaci!"

"What's it all about, boys?" Retief called over the gathering creak and clank as the machines closed in.

"This planet is not your world. We are programed to give no mercies to you."

"Just a minute," Magnan protested. "We're just harmless diplomats. Can't we all be friends or something?"

"Who gave you your order?" Retief asked.

"Our masters," replied a voice like a sand-filled gearbox.

"That was a long time ago," Retief said. "Matters have changed somewhat—"

"Yes, indeed," Magnan chimed in. "You see, now that your old masters are all dead, we're taking over their duties—"

"Our duties are to see you dead," Red-eye boomed, raising a pair of yard-long cleavers.

"Help!" Magnan yelped.

"We wouldn't want to stand in the way of duty," Retief said, watching the poised cutting edges, "but suppose we turned out to be your masters, after all? I'm sure you wouldn't want to make the mistake of slicing up your legitimate owners."

"You see, we took over where they left off," Magnan said hastily. "We're, ah, looking after all their affairs for them, carrying out their wishes as we understand them, tidying up—"

"There is no mistake, Terran. You are not our masters."

"You said masters are better than robots," Retief reminded the machine. "If we can prove our superiority, will you concede the point?"

Silence fell, broken only by the whirr and hum of robotic metabolisms.

"If you could so prove, we will certainly concede your status as our masters," Sand-in-the-gears said at last.

"Gracious, I should think so!" Magnan jerked his rumpled lapels into line. "For a moment, Retief, I confess I was beginning to feel just the teeniest bit apprehensive—"

"You have one minute to prove your superiority," Broken Glass said flatly.

"Well, I should think it was obvious," Magnan sniffed. "Just look at us."

"Indeed, we've done so. We find you little, silly, crude, tender, apprehensive, and harmless."

"You mean—?"

"It means we'll have to do something even more impressive than standing around radiating righteous indignation, Mr. Magnan."

"Well, for heaven's sake," Magnan sniffed. "I never thought I'd see the day when I had to prove the obvious ascendancy of a diplomat over a donkey engine."

"We are waiting," File-on-steel said.

"Well, what do they expect?" Magnan yelped. "It's true they're bigger, stronger, faster, longer-lived, and cheaper to operate; and of course they have vast memory banks and can do lightning calculations and tricks of that sort—which, however, can hardly compare with our unique human ability to, ah, do what we do," he finished in a subdued tone.

"What *do* you do?" Red-eye demanded.

"Why, we, ah, demonstrate moral superiority," Magnan said brightly.

"Shilth was right about your sense of humor," Retief said admiringly. "But I think we'd better defer the subtle jests until we discover whether we're going to survive to enjoy the laugh."

"Well, for heaven's sake, *do* something, Retief," Magnan whispered, "before they make a terrible blunder." He rolled his eyes sideways at a scythe-like implement hovering as if ready to shear at any instant through the volume of space he occupied.

"Time is up," Broken Glass said. The machines surged forward. The scythe, sweeping horizontally, clanged against the descending cleavers as Retief and Magnan jumped aside from the rush of a low-slung tree mower with chattering blades. The latter swerved, collided with a massive punch press, one of whose piston-like members stabbed through the side of a ponderous masonry-wrecker. It wobbled, did a sharp right turn, and slammed into the cast-concrete wall, which cracked and leaned, allowing a massive beam to drop free at one end, narrowly missing Magnan as he rebounded from the flank of a charging garbage-shredder. The falling girder crashed across the midsection of the latter machine with a decisive *crunch!*, pinning the hapless apparatus to the spot. It clashed its treads futilely, sending up a shower of concrete chips. The other machines clustered around it in attitudes of concern, the Terrans for the moment forgotten.

"Hsst! Retief! This is our chance to beat a strategic withdrawal!" Magnan stage-whispered. "If we can just make it back to the elevator—"

"We'll find Shilth waiting at the top," Retief said. "Mr. Magnan, suppose you find a comfortable spot behind a packing case somewhere. I'm not quite ready to leave yet."

"Are you insane? These bloodthirsty bags of bolts are ready to pound us to putty!"

"They seem to be fully occupied with another problem at the moment," Retief pointed out, nodding toward a posthole digger which was fruitlessly poking at the end of the beam which had trapped its fellow. The scythe-armed robot was as busily scraping at the massive member, without result. The ranks parted to let a heavy-duty paint-chipper through; but it merely clattered its chisel tips vainly against the impervious material. And all the while, the pinioned machine groaned lugubriously, sparks flying from its commutator box as it threshed vainly to pull free.

Retief stepped forward; Red-eye swiveled on him, raising a large mallet apparently designed for pounding heavy posts into hard ground.

"Before you drive home your argument," Retief said, "I have a proposal."

"What proposal?"

"You don't seem to be having much luck extricating your colleague from under the beam. Suppose I try—"

"One minute. I will lift the beam," a deep voice boomed. A massively built loading robot trundled forward, maneuvered deftly into position, secured a grip on the concrete member with its single huge arm and heaved. For a moment, nothing happened; then there was a sharp *clonk!* and a broken duralloy torque rod dangled from the lifter's forged-steel biceps. The girder had not stirred.

"Tough luck, old fellow," Retief said. "My turn."

"Good heavens, Retief, if that cast-iron Hercules couldn't do it, how can you hope to succeed?" Magnan squeaked from his corner.

"You have the ability to help our colleague?" Broken Glass demanded.

"If I do, will you follow my orders?"

"If you can do that which we cannot do, your superiority is obvious."

"In that case, just pull that bar out of there, will you?" Retief pointed to a four-inch-diameter steel rod, twenty feet long, part of a roller assembly presumably once used in loading operations. A stacking machine gripped the rod and gave it a firm pull, ripping it free from its mountings.

"Stick one end under the edge of the beam, like a

70

good fellow," Retief said. "You there, jackhammer: Push that anvil under the rod, eh?" The machines complied with his requests with brisk efficiency, adjusting the lever as directed, with the fulcrum as close as possible to the weight to be lifted.

"Retief—if you couldn't even lift the lever, how are you going to . . ." Magnan's voice faded as Retief stepped up on the tread-skirt of a sand-blaster and put a foot on the up-angled long arm of the jury-rigged prybar. Steadying himself, he let his full weight onto the rod. Instantly, it sank gracefully down, lifting the multiton beam a full half inch from the depression it had imprinted in the garbage-shredder. The latter made a clanking sound, attempted to move, emitted a cascade of electrical sputterings, and subsided.

"He's ruptured himself!" Magnan gasped. "Poor thing. Still, we've done our part."

The other machines were maneuvering, making way for a squat cargo-tug, which backed up to the victim but was unable to get in position to attach its tow cable. A dirt-pusher with a wide blade tried next, but in the close quarters failed to get within six feet of the disabled machine. The others had no better luck.

"Mr. Magnan, find a length of cable," Retief called. Magnan rummaged, turned up a rusting coil of braided wire.

"One of you robots with digits, tie one end of the cable to the patient," Retief said. "Cinch the other up to something that won't give."

Two minutes later the cable was stretched drumtight from a massive stanchion to the cripple, running between closely spaced paired columns.

"Next, we apply a transverse pull to the center of the cable," Retief directed.

"They can't," Magnan wailed. "There's no room!"

"In that case, Mr. Magnan, perhaps you'd be good enough to perform the office."

"I?" Magnan's eyebrows went up. "Perhaps you've forgotten my motorman's arm."

"Use the other one."

"You expect me, one-handed, to budge that ten-ton hulk?"

"Better hurry up, sir. I feel my foot slipping."

"This is madness," Magnan exclaimed, but he stepped to the cable, gripped it at midpoint, and tugged. With a harsh squeak of metal, the damaged machine moved forward half an inch.

"Why—why, that's positively astonishing!" Magnan said with a pleased look.

"Tighten the cable and do it again!" Retief said quickly. The machines hurried to take up the slack. Magnan, with an amazed expression, applied a second pull. The wreck moved another centimeter. After three more nibbles, the tug was able to hook on and drag its fellow clear. Retief jumped down, letting the beam drop with a floor-shaking *boom!*

"Heavens!" Magnan found his voice. "I never imagined I was such a brute! After all, the diplomatic life *is* somewhat sedentary . . ." He flexed a thin arm, fingering it in search of a biceps.

"Wrestling with the conscience is excellent exercise," Retief pointed out. "And you've held up your end of some rather weighty conversations in your time."

"Jape if you must," Magnan said coolly. "But you can't deny I *did* free the creature—er, machine, that is."

"You have freed our colleague," Sand-in-the-gears said to Magnan. "We are waiting for your orders, Master."

"To be sure." Magnan placed his fingertips together and pursed his lips. "You won't fit into the lift," he said judiciously, looking over his new subjects. "Is there another way up?"

"To be sure, Master."

"Excellent. I want all of you to ascend to the surface at once, round up and disarm every Groaci on the planet, and lock them up. And see that you don't squash the one called Shilth in the process. I have a little gloating to do."

4

On a newly excavated terrace under a romantically crumbling wall of pink brick, Magnan and Retief sat with Shilth, the latter wearing a crestfallen expression involving quivering anterior mandibles and drooping eyestalks. His elaborate cloak of office was gone, and there were smudges of axle grease on his once-polished thorax.

"Dirty pool, Magnan," the Groaci said, his breathy voice fainter than ever. "I was in line for the Order of the Rubber Calipers, Second Class, at the very least, and you spoiled it all with your perambulating junkyard. Who would have dreamed you'd been so sly as to secretly conceal a host of war machines? I suspect you did it merely to embarrass me."

"Actually," Magnan began, and paused. "Actually, it *was* quite shrewd of me, now that you mention it."

"I think you overdid the camouflage, however," Shilth said acidly as a street broom whiffled past, casting a shower of dust over the party. "The confounded things don't appear to be aware that the coup is over. They're still carrying on the charade."

"I like to keep my lads occupied," Magnan said briskly, nodding grandly at a hauler trundling past along the newly cleaned avenue with a load of newly uprooted brush. "Helps to keep them in trim in case they're needed suddenly to quell any disturbances."

"Never fear. I've impressed on Thish that he will not long survive any threat to my well-being."

"Company coming," Retief said, gesturing toward a descending point of sun-bright blue light. They watched the ship settle into a landing a quarter of a mile distant, then rose and strolled over to greet the emerging passengers.

"Why, it's Mr. Pennyfool," Magnan said. "I knew he'd be along to rescue us. Yoo-hoo, Mr. Penny-fool . . ."

"That's Mr. Ambassador, Magnan," Pennyfool corrected sharply. "Kindly step aside. You're interfering with a delicate negotiation." The little man marched past Retief without a glance, halted before Shilth, offering a wide smile and a limp hand. The Groaci studied the latter, turned it over gingerly and examined the back, then dropped it.

"Liver spots," he said. "How unaesthetic."

"Now, Planetary Director Shilth, we're prepared to offer a handsome fee in return for exploratory lights here on Verdigris." Pennyfool restored his smile with an effort. "Of course, anything we find will be turned over to you at once—"

"Oh, ah, Mr. Ambassador," Magnan hazarded.

"We Groaci," Shilth said sourly, "are not subject to such pigmentational disorders. We remain a uniform, soothing puce at all times."

"Sir," Magnan piped up, "I'd just like—"

"Now, naturally, we're prepared to underwrite a generous program of planetary development to assist your people in settling in," Pennyfool hurried on. "I had in mind about half a billion to start . . ." He paused to gauge reaction. "Per year, of course," he amended, judging the omens, "with adequate bonuses

74

for special projects, naturally. Now, I'd say a staff of, say, two hundred to begin with . . . ?"

"Pennyfool, I have a dreadful node-ache," Shilth hissed. "Why don't you go jump down an elevator shaft?" He patted back a counterfeit yawn and stalked away.

"Well, I can see that this is going to be a challenge," Pennyfool said, staring after the alien. "The tricky fellow is going to hold out for two billion, no doubt."

"Mr. Ambassador, I have good news," Magnan said hastily. "We can save the taxpayers those billions. Verdigris belongs to me!"

"See here, Magnan, the privation can't have scrambled your meager wits already! You've only been here seventy-two hours!"

"But, sir—there's no need to promise Shilth the moon—"

"Aha! So that's what he's holding out for. Well, I see no reason the negotiation should founder over a mere satellite—" Pennyfool turned to pursue Shilth.

"No, no, you don't quite grasp my meaning," Magnan yipped, grabbing at his superior's sleeve.

"Unhand me, Magnan!" Pennyfool roared. "I'll see to your release after other, more vital matters are dealt with. In the meantime, I suggest you set a good example by cobbling a record number of shoes, or whatever task they've set you—"

"Master, is this person troubling you?" a torn-metal voice inquired. Magnan and Pennyfool whirled to see a rust-covered hedge clipper looming over them, four-foot clippers at the ready.

"No, that's quite all right, Albert," Magnan said acidly. "I *like* being bullied."

"You're quite certain you don't wish him trimmed to a uniform height?"

"No—I just want him to listen to what I have to say."

Albert clacked the shears together with a nerve-shredding sound.

"I—I'd love to listen to you, my dear Magnan," Pennyfool said rapidly.

Magnan delivered a brief account of his capture of the planet. "So you see, sir," he concluded, "the whole thing is Terran property."

"Magnan!" Pennyfool roared, then with a glance at Albert, lowered his voice to a whisper. "Do you realize what this means? When I reported the Groaci here ahead of us, I was appointed as Terran Ambassador Extraordinary and Minister Plenipotentiary to the confounded place! If we own it, then *pfft!* There goes my appointment!"

"Great heavens, sir"—Magnan paled at the announcement—"I had no idea . . ."

"Look here, do you suppose we could get them to take it back?"

"What, stay here, surrounded by these mobile, moldy monstrosities?" Shilth, who had returned silently, hissed. "Never! I demand repatriation!"

Retief caught Magnan's eye as Pennyfool turned to soothe the Groaci.

"What is it, Retief? Can't you see I'm at a critical point, careerwise?"

"I have a suggestion," Retief said.

As Magnan rejoined Pennyfool, Shilth was still hissing imprecations.

"Master, what say I prune this fellow a bit," Albert proposed. "He seems to have sprouted too many eyes."

"Not unless he says another word," Magnan said. He turned to Pennyfool with a thoughtful look. "I say, sir, suppose I should come up with a scheme which will insure your confirmation, and which will at the same time reflect favorably on the Terran image: you know, the kindly, selfless, helping-hand sort of thing . . . ?"

"Yes, yes?"

"I daresay, once established here, you'd want to surround yourself with a staff widely versed in local problems—"

"Naturally. There are plenty of reliable team men available doing Underground research work in subterranean libraries back at Sector. Get on with it, Magnan."

"I want the Counselorship," Magnan said crisply.

"You, number two man in my Embassy? Ridiculous! I'd have to jump you over the heads of men with vast experience under their belts!"

"Most of my experience has been at a somewhat higher level," Magnan said loftily. "No Counselorship, no scheme."

"What's this, Magnan, blackmail?" Pennyfool gasped.

"Precisely," Magnan said.

Pennyfool opened his mouth to yell, then closed it and nodded.

"Magnan, it's apparent you're more familiar with the techniques of diplomacy than I suspected. I accept. Now, just what do you have in mind . . . ?"

5

"It's a bit unusual," Ambassador Pennyfool said complacently, glancing out the window of his freshly refurbished office on the top floor of a newly excavated tower of green anodized aluminum serving as

CDT Chancery. "But on the other hand, its uniqueness offers a certain challenge."

"Gracious yes," Counselor Magnan said, nodding. "The first Terran envoy to present credentials to a mechanical Head of State."

"I don't know," the Military Attaché said darkly. "Freeing these inanimate objects and letting them set up in business for themselves may create a dangerous precedent. What if cybernetic military equipment, for example, should start getting ideas about pensions and promotions?"

"And office machines," the Budget and Fiscal Officer said worriedly. "If my bookkeeping computers took it into their transistors to start agitating for civil rights, I shudder to contemplate the consequences in terms of, say, late paychecks."

"I'm already having trouble with my Motor Pool picking up liberal ideas," the Admin Officer wagged his head, frowning. "I've had to enact strict rules against fraternization with the natives."

There was a musical chime from the desk screen. The square-cornered sense-organ panel of Planetary President Albert Sand-in-the-gears appeared.

"Ah, there, Pennyfool," the robotic Chief of State said in a tone as genial as his vocal equipment would allow, "I hoped I'd find you in. I was just ringing up to ask whether you'd care to join me on the links this afternoon for a few holes of ballistic golf."

"I'm sorry, Mr. President," the Terran said shortly. "A game in which one is required to score eight holes-in-one out of ten from a tee seven miles from the green is not my strong suit."

"Of course. I keep forgetting you're not equipped with telescopic sights. A pity." The President sighed, a sound like tearing steel. "It was difficult enough grasping the idea of the superiority of my inferiors;

78

trying to behave as equals is even more trying—no offense intended, of course."

"Mr. President—who's that sitting behind you?" Pennyfool asked sharply.

"Ah, forgive me. This is Special Trade Representative Shilth, of Groac. His government has sent him along to assist in getting the Verdigian economy rolling."

"How long has *he* been here?"

"Long enough to demonstrate my indispensability." Shilth leaned forward to leer at the Terrans. "I've already concluded trade agreements with a number of hard-currency markets for export of Verdigian antiquities—"

"You didn't!" Pennyfool gasped.

"Oh, have no fear; they're not the real thing." Shilth waggled an eye at Magnan, who pretended not to notice. "Tho' we let it be noised about that they're all bootleg national treasures."

"Oh, I see. Reproductions." Pennyfool grunted. "Just so you don't ship any irreplaceable *objects d'art* offplanet."

"We won't. We require them as patterns for the matter duplicators."

"Eh?"

"The locals are digging them out by the truckload; they sort them, discard the rejects—broken pots and the like—then scrub up the choice items and send them along to the duplication centers. We already have a dozen plants in full swing. Our ceramic fingering knobs are already a sensation with the cultured set. In a year, Verdigris will be known as the antique capital of the Eastern Arm."

"Matter duplicators? You're flooding the Galaxy with bogus antiques?"

"Bogus? They're identical with the real thing, to the last molecule."

"Hah! The genuine articles are priceless examples of Verdigrian art; the copies are just so much junk!"

"But, my dear Pennyfool—if one can't distinguish a masterpiece from a piece of junk . . . ?"

"*I* can detect the genuine at a glance!"

"Show me," the Groaci said, and whipped out a pair of seemingly identical shapes of lumpy blue-glazed clay the size and approximate shape of stunted rutabagas.

". . . but, unfortunately, I have something in my eye." Pennyfool subsided, poking at the offending organ.

"A pity. I would have enjoyed a demonstration of your expertise," Shilth cooed.

"Well, gentlemen, that tears it," the Ambassador said to his staff after the screen had blanked. "After all my delicate maneuvering to secure self-determination for these unfortunate relics of a bygone age, and to place the CDT in a position of paternal influence vis-à-vis their emergent nation, the infernal Groaci have stolen a march on us again. Fake antiques, indeed!"

"Goodness, I see what you mean, Mr. Ambassador," Magnan said sympathetically. "Why didn't *we* think of doing that?"

In the Chancery corridor ten minutes later, Magnan mopped at his thin neck with a large floral-patterned tissue.

"Heavens, who'd have thought he'd fly into such a passion?" he inquired of Retief. "After all, it isn't as if those silly little gobs of mud possessed any intrinsic merit."

"Oh, I don't know," Retief said. "They're not bad, considering that the locals have to mass-produce them and bury them at night when nobody's looking."

"Retief!" Magnan stopped dead. "You don't mean . . . ?"

"It seemed like a good idea to sidetrack the Groaci away from the genuine stuff," Retief pointed out. "Just in case any of it had any sentimental value."

"Fake fakes," Magnan murmured. "The concept has a certain euphony."

They paused beside a pair of double glass doors opening onto an airy balcony two hundred feet above the freshly scrubbed city. As they stepped out, a small copter with a saddle and handlebars came winging in across the park to hover just beyond the balustrade.

"Hop aboard, Retief, we're late," the machine called in a cheerful baritone.

"Retief, where are you going?" Magnan barked as the latter swung over the rail. "You have the quarterly Report of Redundant Reports to compile, to say nothing of the redundant reports themselves . . . !"

"Duty calls, Mr. Magnan," Retief said soothingly. "I'm off to a game of sky polo with a couple of Cabinet Ministers." He waved and set spurs to his mount, which launched itself with a bound into the wide green sky.

Pime Doesn't Cray

A driving rain lashed the tarmac as Retief stepped from the shuttlecraft that had ferried him down to the planetary surface. From the direction of the low, mushroom-shaped reception sheds, a slight figure wrapped in a voluminous black rubber poncho came splashing toward him, waving excitedly.

"You got any enemies, Mac?" the shuttle pilot asked nervously, watching the newcomer's approach.

"A reasonable number," Retief replied, drawing on his cigar, which sputtered and hissed as the rain struck the glowing tip. "However, this is just Counselor Magnan from the Embassy, here to welcome me to the scene with the local disaster status, no doubt.'"

"No time to waste, Retief," Magnan panted as he came up. "Ambassador Grossblunder's called a special staff meeting for five pee em-half an hour from now. If we hurry, we can just make it. I've already seen to Customs and Immigration; I knew you'd want to be there, to, er—"

"Share the blame?" Retief suggested.

"Hardly," Magnan corrected, flicking a drop of moisture from the tip of his nose. "As a matter of fact, I may well be in a line for a word of praise for my handling of the Cultural Aid Project. It will be an excellent opportunity for you to get your feet wet, local scenewise," he amplified, leading the way toward the Embassy car waiting beside the sheds.

"According to the latest supplement to the Post Report," Retief said as they settled themselves against the deep-pile upholstery, "the project is scheduled for completion next week. Nothing's gone wrong with the timetable, I hope?"

Magnan leaned forward to rap at the glass partition dividing the enclosed passenger compartment from the open-air driver's seat; the chauffeur, a rather untidy-looking local who seemed to consist of a snarl of purple macaroni topped by a peaked cap with a shiny bill, angled what Retief deduced to be an ear to catch the Terran's instructions.

"Just swing past the theater on your way down, Chauncey," Magnan directed. "In answer to your question," he said complacently to Retief, "I don't mind saying the project went off flawlessly, hitchwise. In fact, it's completed a week early. As Project Director, I fancy it's something of a feather in my cap, considering the frightful weather conditions we have to contend with here on Squale."

"Did you say 'theater'? As I recall, the original proposal called for the usual Yankee Stadium-type sports arena."

Magnan smiled loftily. "I thought it time to vary the program."

"Congratulations, Mr. Magnan." Retief sketched a salute with his cigar. "I was afraid the *Corps Diplomatique* was going to go on forever inflicting bigger and better baseball diamonds on defenseless natives, while the Groaci countered with ever larger and uglier Bolshoi-type ballet arenas."

"Not this time," Magnan stated with satisfaction. "I've beaten the scamps at their own game. This is Top Secret, mind you—but this time *we've* built the Bolshoi-type ballet theater!"

"A masterful gambit, Mr. Magnan. How are the Groaci taking it?"

"Hmmph. They've come up with a rather ingenious counterstroke, I must concede. Informed opinion has it the copycats are assembling an imitation Yankee Stadium in reprisal." Magnan peered out through the downpour. The irregularly shaped buildings lining the winding avenue loomed mistily, obscured by sheets of wind-driven precipitation. Ahead, a gap in their orderly ranks was visible. Magnan frowned as the car cruised slowly past a large, irregularly shaped bulk set well back from the curb.

"Here, Chauncey," he called, "I instructed you to drive to the project site!"

"Thure shing, moss-ban," a voice like a clogged drain replied placatingly. "Weer we har."

"Chauncey—have you been drinking?"

"Woe, nurse luck." Chauncey braked to a stop; the windshield wipers rotated busily; the air cushion sighed heavily, driving ripples across the puddled street. "Book, loss—were right astreet the cross from the Libric Publary, *nicht vahr?*"

"The Lublic Pibrary, you mean—I mean the pubic lilberry—"

"Yeah, mats what I thean. So—there's the piblary —so buts the weef?" Chauncey extended the cluster of macaroni that served as his hand, to wave like seaweed in a light current.

"Visibility is simply atrocious here on Squale," Magnan sniffed, rolling down the window and recoiling as a blast of rain splattered his face. "But even so

—I shouldn't think I could get confused as to the whereabouts of my own project . . ."

"It looks like a collapsed circus tent," Retief commented, studying the half acre of canvas apparently supported by half a dozen randomly placed props.

"An optical illusion," Magnan said firmly. "The structure is under wraps, of course; it's a secret, you know. It's just the lighting, no doubt, that makes it look so . . . so sort of squatty and unplanned . . ." He was squinting ferociously into the rain, shading his eyes with a hand. "Still, why don't we just pop out and have a closer look?"

Magnan thrust the door open and stumbled out; Retief followed. They crossed a walk of colored, glazed tile, skirted a bed of foot-wide green blossoms. Magnan lifted aside a fold of plastic sheeting, revealing a yawning excavation at the bottom of which severed electrical and plumbing connections poked up through the surface of the muddy water pooling there.

"A treat nick," Chauncey said admiringly over his shoulder. "Do'd you how it, Master Mignan?"

"Do'd I how what?" Magnan croaked.

"Dis it makappear," Chauncey amplified. "The meaning, I build."

"Retief," Magnan whispered, blinking hard. "Tell me I'm seeing things; I mean, that I'm *not* seeing things."

"Correct," Retief said, "either way you phrase it."

"Retief," Magnan said in a breaking voice, "do you realize what this means?"

Retief tossed his cigar down into the empty pit, where it hissed and went out. "Either you were kidding me about the project—"

"I assure you—"

"—or we're standing on the wrong corner—"

"Absolutely not!"

"Or someone," Retief said, "has stolen one each Bolshoitype ballet theater."

<h1 style="text-align:center">2</h1>

"And I was dreaming of feathers in my cap," Magnan moaned as the car braked to a halt before the imposing façade of the Terrestrial Embassy. "I'll be fortunate to salvage my cap from this fiasco—or my head, for that matter. How will I ever tell Ambassador Grossblunder I've misplaced his pet project?"

"Oh, I'm sure you'll be able to pass the incident off with your usual *savoir-faire*," Retief soothed, as they stepped out into the drizzle. The Sqalian doorman, loosely packed in a regulation CDT-issue coverall, nodded a cluster of writhing violet-hued filaments at the Terrans as they came up.

"Jowdy, hents," he said as the door whooshed open. "Rice nain, eh?"

"What's so rice about it?" Magnan inquired acidly. "Harvey—has His Excellency gone in?"

"Men tinutes ago—in a masty nude. Didn't even hey sello."

Inside, Magnan put a hand to his brow. "Retief—I seem to have just come down with a splitting headache. Why don't you nip along and mention this development just casually to the Ambassador. Possibly you could play it down a trifle. No need to upset him unduly, eh?"

"Good idea, Mr. Magnan," Retief said, handing his weather cape into the check room. "I'll hint that it's all a publicity trick you dreamed up to publicize the grand opening."

"Excellent notion! And if you could subtly plant

the idea that you'll have it back in place in time for the festivities . . ." Magnan looked hopefully at Retief.

"Since I just arrived fifteen minutes ago, I think that would be rather pushy of me. Then too, he might want to know why you were lying down at such a critical moment in Terran/Squalian relations."

Magnan groaned again, resignedly.

"Let's hurry along, gentlemen," a short, black-eyebrowed man in uniform called from the open elevator door across the lobby. "We're holding the car for you."

Magnan straightened his narrow shoulders. "Coming, Colonel Otherday," he croaked. "Remember, Retief," he added in an undertone, "we'll behave as though it were the most natural thing in the world for a ten-million-credit building to vanish between breakfast and lunch."

"Did I hear someone mention lunch?" a portly diplomat inquired from the back of the car.

"You just ate, Lester," a lean Commercial Attaché said. "As for you, Mr. Retief, you picked an inauspicious moment to put in an appearance; I gather the Ambassador's in a towering pet this evening."

Magnan glanced nervously at Retief. "Ah—any idea what's troubling His Excellency . . . ?" he inquired of the car in general.

"Who knows?" the Attaché shrugged. "Last time it was a deteriorating man/bean ratio in the Embassy snack bar."

"This time it's even bigger than the bean crisis," Colonel Otherday stated flatly. "I have a feeling this time heads will roll."

"Does it have anything to do with, ah, anything that might be, er, missing?" Magnan inquired with an attempt at casualness.

"Ah-hah!" the lean Attaché pounced. "He knows something, gentlemen!"

"Come on, Magnan," the portly First Secretary urged. "Let us in on it."

"How is it you always have the word first?" the Colonel inquired plaintively.

"Well, as to that," Magnan started—

"Mr. Magnan is under oath to reveal nothing, gentlemen," Retief cut in smoothly as the car halted and the doors slid back on a wide, deep-carpeted conference room.

A long, polished table occupied the center of the floor, unadorned but for long yellow pads and ballpoint pens at each place. A few seconds of unobtrusive scuffling ensued as the diplomats, all veteran campaigners, vied for choice positions, balancing the prestige of juxtaposition to the Ambassadorial chair against nonconspicuousness in the event of scapegoat selection.

All hands stood as the inner door was flung wide; the stern-visaged, multichinned figure of Ambassador Grossblunder entered the room under full sail. He scanned the assembled bureaucrats without visible approval, seated himself in the chair the Agricultural Attaché leaped to pull out, shot a piercing glance along the table, cleared his throat.

"Lock the doors," he said. "Gentlemen, be seated. I have solemn news for you." He paused impressively. "We," he concluded solemnly, "have been robbed!"

A sigh passed along the table; all eyes swiveled to Magnan.

"Robbed!" Grossblunder repeated, emphasizing the point with a blow of his fist which made the pencils, plus a number of the diplomats, jump. "I have for some time suspected that foul play was afoot; a short time ago my worst fears were confirmed. Gentlemen, there is a thief among us!"

"Among *us?*" Magnan blurted. "But how—I mean, why—that is to say—Mr. Ambassador—how could one of *us* have, er, purloined the, ah, loot in question?"

"You may well ask! One might also logically inquire as to why any person connected with this Mission could so far forget himself as to hide the feet that banns him! That is, bite the fan that heeds him. I mean beat the hide that fans him. Confound it, you know what I mean!" Grossblunder grabbed a glass of water and gulped a swallow. "Been here too long," he muttered. "Losing my grasp of the well-rounded period."

"A thief, you say, sir," Colonel Otherday prompted. "Well, how interesting . . ."

" 'Interesting' is hardly the word for it," Grossblunder barked, " 'Appalling' is a cut nearer the mark. 'Shocking,' though a trifle flaccid, carries a portion of the connotation. This is a grievous blot on the CDT copybook, gentlemen! A blow stuck at the very foundations of Galactic accord!"

A chorus of "Right, Chief's!" and "Well phrased, sir's," and a lone "You said it, Boss," from the Press Attaché provided counterpoint to the plenipotentiary's pronouncement.

"Now, if anyone here wishes to come forward at this juncture . . ." Grossblunder's ominous gaze traveled along the table, lingered on Magnan.

"You appear to be the focal point of all eyes, Magnan," the Ambassador accused. "If you've a comment, don't hesitate. Speak up!"

"Why, as a matter of fact, sir," Magnan gulped, "I just wanted to say that, as for myself, I was utterly appalled—that is to say, shocked—when I discovered the loss. Why, you could have knocked me over with the feather in my cap—I mean—"

Grossblunder looked ominous. "You're saying you were already aware of the pilferage, Magnan?"

"Yes, and—"

"And failed to confide this intelligence in me?" the Ambassador glowered.

"I didn't actually *know* until a few minutes ago," Magnan explained hastily. "Why, gracious, sir, you were positive *miles* ahead of me! It's just that I'm able to confirm your revelation—not that any confirmation is needed, of course." He paused to gulp.

"Now, *there,* gentlemen," Grossblunder said with admiration, "is my conception of an alert officer. While the rest of you went about your business oblivious of the light fingers operating to the detriment of this Mission, my Counselor, Mr. Magnan, alone among my subordinates, sensed mischief afoot! Congratulations to you, sir!"

"Why, ah, thank you, Mr. Ambassador," Magnan essayed a fragile smile. "I *do* try to keep abreast of developments—"

"And since you seem to have the matter in hand, you're appointed Investigative Officer, to get to the bottom of the matter without delay. I'll turn my records over to you without further ado." Grossblunder shot his cuff, allotted a glance to his watch. "As it happens, my VIP copter is at this moment warming up on the roof to whisk me over to the Secretariat, where I expect to be tied up for the remainder of the evening in high-level talks with the Foreign Minister regarding slurb-fruit allocations for the coming fiscal quarter. It seems our Groaci colleagues are out to cut us out of the pattern luxury-tradewise, a consummation hardly to be tolerated on my record." He rose. "You'll accompany me to the helipad, Magnan, for last-minute briefing. As for the rest of you—let Magnan's performance stand as an example. You there—" He pointed at Retief. "You may carry my briefcase."

On the roof—aslosh with rainwater under the perpetually leaden sky—Grossblunder turned to Magnan.

"I expect fast action, Ben. We can't allow this sort of thing to pass unnoticed, as it were."

"I'll do my best, sir," Magnan chirped. "And I do want to say it's awfully white of you not to hold me personally responsible—not that anyone could actually *blame* me, of course—"

"*You* responsible? Hmmm. No, I see no way in which I could benefit from that. Beside which," he added, "you're not an Admin man."

"Admin man, sir? What . . . ?"

"My analysis of the records indicates that a steady trickle over the past two years at the present rate could account for a total discrepancy on the order of sixty-seven gross! Think of that, Magnan!"

"Sixty-seven Bolshoi-type ballet theaters?" Magnan quavered.

Grossblunder blinked, then allowed a smile to quirk a corner of his mouth. "No need to hint, Magnan. I haven't forgotten your magnificent performance in the completion of the project six days ahead of schedule. The grand opening tomorrow is the one bright spot on my Effectiveness Report—on my horizon, that is to say. I wouldn't be surprised if there were a citation in store for the officer responsible." He winked, then frowned. "But don't allow the prospect to drive the matter of the missing paperclips into eclipse! I want action!"

"P—paperclips, sir?"

"A veritable torrent of them, dropped from Embassy records as expendable items! Outrageous! But no need to say more, my boy; you're as aware as I of the seriousness of the situation." Grossblunder gripped his junior's thin shoulder. "Remember, Magnan—I'm counting on you!" He turned and clambered into his seat; with a rising flutter of rotors, the light machine lifted into the overcast and was gone. Magnan turned shakily to Retief.

"I . . . I thought . . . I thought he knew . . ."

"I know," Retief commiserated. "Still, you can always pick an opportune time to tell him later. While he's pinning the medal on, perhaps."

"How can you jest at such a moment? Do you realize that I have to solve not one, but two crimes, before the Ambassador and the Minister finish a bottle of port?"

"That's a thought; maybe you can get a quantity discount. Still, we'd better get started before they run the ante up any higher."

3

Back in his office, Magnan found awaiting him a letter bearing the Great Seal of the Groacian Autonomy.

"It's an *Aide Mémoire* from that wretch, Ambassador Shinth," he told Retief. "Announcing he's moving the date for the unveiling of his Cultural Aid project up to midnight tonight!" He groaned, tossed the note aside. "This is the final blow, Retief! And I, without so much as a kiosk to offer in rebuttal!"

"I understood the Groaci were behind schedule," Retief said.

"They are! This entire affair is impossible, Retief! No one could have stolen a complete building overnight—and if they had, where would they hide it? And even if they found a place to hide it—and we were able to turn it up—how in the world would we

92

·get it back in position in time for a ceremony scheduled less than twenty hours local from this moment?"

"That covers the questions," Retief said. "We may have a little more trouble with the answers."

"The building was there last night; I stopped to admire the classical neon meander adorning the architrave on my way home. A splendid effect; Shinth would have been green with envy—or whatever color Groaci diplomats turn when confronted with an aesthetic coup of such proportions."

"He may be quietly turning puce with satisfaction at this moment," Retief suggested. "Rather neat timing: his project ready to go, and ours missing."

"How will I ever face Shinth?" Magnan was muttering. "Only last night I assayed a number of sly jests at his expense. I thought at the time he took it rather blandly—" Magnan broke off to stare at Retief. "Great heavens!" he gasped. "Are you hinting those sneaky little five-eyed Meyer-come-latelies could have so far abused diplomatic practice as to be behind this outrage?"

"The thought had crossed my mind," Retief admitted. "Offhand, I can't think of anyone else who might have a yen for a Bolshoi-type ballet theater."

Magnan leaped up, yanking the pale-mauve lapels of his early midafternoon hemi-demi-informal cutaway into place. "Of course!" he cried. "Call out the Marine Guard, Retief! I'll march right up to that underhanded little weasel and demand the return of the purloined edifice on the spot!"

"Better be careful what spot you're on," Retief cautioned. "A Bolshoi-type ballet theater occupies a full block, remember."

"An ill-timed jape, Retief," Magnan snapped. "Well, what are you waiting for?" He paused, frowning. "Am I to deduce from your apparent lack of enthusiasm that you see some flaw in the scheme?"

93

"Just a small one," Retief said. "His Groacian Excellency has probably covered his tracks quite carefully. He'll laugh in your face—unless you can show some proof."

"Not even Shinth would have the cheek to deny the facts if I catch him red-handed!" Magnan paused, looking troubled. "Of course, I haven't actually found any evidence yet . . ." He nipped at a hangnail and cast a sidelong glance at Retief.

"A ballet theater isn't the easiest thing in the world to hide," Retief said. "Suppose we try to turn it up first; then we can start on the problem of how to get it back."

"Good notion, Retief. Just what I was about to suggest." Magnan looked at the watch on his thumb. "Why don't you just pop round and have a look here and there, while I whip my paperwork into shape; then after dinner we can get together and agree on a story—formulate a report, that is, indicating we've done everything possible."

Leaving the Counselor's office, Retief went along to the Commercial Section. A chinless clerk looked up from among baled newspaper clippings. "Hi, there, Mr. Retief. I see you made it. Welcome to Squale."

"Thanks, Freddy; I'd like to see a listing of all cargoes imported by the Groaci Embassy during the last twelve months."

The clerk poked the keys of the data bank, frowned at the list it disgorged.

"Flimsy construction they must have in mind," he said as he handed it over. "Cardboard and pick-up sticks. Typical."

"Anything else?" Reteif persisted.

"I'll check equipment imports." The clerk tapped out another code, eliciting a brief clatter and a second slip of paper.

"Heavy-duty lift units," he said. "Funny. They

don't need heavy-duty units to handle plywood and two-by's . . ."

"Four of them," Retief noted. "With wide-aperture fields and gang interlocks."

"Wow! With that, you could pick up the Squalid-Hilton."

"You could, indeed," Retief agreed. "Thanks, Freddy."

Outside, it was dusk; the car was waiting at the curb. Retief directed Chauncey to drive back along the wet, tree-fern-shaded avenues to the vacant edge-of-town site so recently occupied by the stolen building. Stepping out into the steady, warm rain, he entered the tent, circled the yawning excavation, studying the soft ground by the beam of a hand light.

"Look are you whatting for?" Chauncey inquired, ambling along behind him on feet that resembled dishpan-sized wads of wet magenta yarn. "Ardon my pasking, but I taught you Therries lidn't dike feeting your get wet."

"Just getting the lie of the land, Chauncey," Retief said. "It appears that whoever pinched the theater lifted it out of here with grav units—probably intact, since there doesn't seem to be any evidence of disassembly."

"I goant dett you, chief," Chauncey said. "You lawk tight this roll houtine isn't trust a jick Master Mignan add off to pulvertise the And Gropening."

"Perish the thought, Chauncey; it's just my way of heightening the suspense." Retief stooped, picked up a pinkish dope-stick butt, sniffed at it. It gave off the sharp odor of ether characteristic of Groaci manufacture.

"We Squalians are no runch of boobs, you understand," Chauncey went on "We've treen a few sicks in our time. If you howns want to clam it up, that's jake;

jut bust betwoon the tea of us—how the heck dood he dee it?"

"I'm afraid that's a diplomatic secret," Retief said. "Let's go take a look at the Groaci answer to our cultural challenge."

"Mot nuch to owe seever there," the local said disparagingly as they squelched back to the car, idling on its air cushion above a wide puddle. "Guthing knowing on; and if were thuzz, you shouldn't key it; they got this buy ford hence aplound the race, and a tunch of barps everying coverthing up."

"The Groaci are a secretive group," Retief said. "But maybe we can get a peek anyway."

"I bon't know, doss; there's a gunch of bards around there, too—with yuns, get. They don't clett lobody net goase."

Steering through the rain-sleek streets under the celery-like trees, Chauncey hummed a sprightly little tune, sounding first like a musical comb, then a rubber-stringed harp, ending with a blatter like a bursting bagpipe.

"Bot nad, hey?" he solicited a compliment, "all but that cast lord; it was subeezed to poe a tourish of flumpets, but my slinger fipped."

"Very impressive," Retief said. "How are you on woodwinds?"

"So-so," Chauncey said. "I'm stretter on bings. Vile this getolin effect." He extruded an arm, quickly arranged four thin filaments along it, and drew a hastily improvised member across the latter, eliciting a shrill bleat.

"Gutty pred, hey? I can't tay any plunes yet, but I lactice a prot; I'll pet it down gat in toe nime."

"Groaci nose-flute lovers will come over to you in a body," Retief predicted. "By the way, Chauncey, how long have the Groaci been working on their ballpark?"

"Lell, wet's see: Stay tharted it fast lall, bust ajout the time too Yerries foured your poundations . . ."

"It must be about finished, eh?"

"It hasn't changed such mince the worst feak; and a thunny fing: You sever seem to knee any jerkers around the wob; gust the jards." Chauncey swung the corner and pulled up before a ten-foot-high fence constructed of closely fitted plastic panels, looming darkly in the early-evening gloom.

"Ear we har," he said. "Sike I lezz, you san't key a thing."

"Let's take a look around."

"Sure—but we petter beep an eye keeled; those dittle levels can squeak up awful niet."

Leaving the car parked in a pool of shadow under the spreading fronds of a giant fern, Retief, followed by the Squalian, strolled along the walk, studying the unbroken wall that completely encircled the block. At the corner he paused, looked both ways. The street lamp glowed mistily on empty sidewalks.

"Give me a chord on the cello if you see anyone coming," Retief directed Chauncey. He extracted a slender instrument from an inner pocket, forced it between two planks, and twisted. The material yielded with a creak, opening a narrow peephole, affording a view of pole-mounted lights which shed a yellowish glow on a narrow belt of foot-trampled mud stacked with two-by-fours and used plywood, a fringe of ragged grass ending at a vertical escarpment of dun-colored canvas. A giant tarpaulin, held in place by a network of ropes, completely concealed the massive structure beneath it.

"Moley hoses," Chauncey's voice sounded at Retief's elbow. "Looks like they've been chaking some manges!"

"What kind of changes?"

"Well—it's sard of hay, tunder that arp—shut the

97

bape of it dooks lifferent. Wave been thirking on it, no bout adout that."

"Suppose we cruise over and pay a call at the Groaci Embassy," Retief suggested. "There are one or two more points that need clearing up."

"Boor, shoss—but it don't woo you any good. They pard that glace like it was the legendary Nort Fox."

"I'm counting on it, Chauncey."

It was a ten-block drive through rain-soaked streets. They parked a block from the fortresslike structure, prowled closer, keeping to the shadows. A pair of Groaci in elaborate uniforms stood stiffly flanking the gate in the high masonry wall.

"No hole-poking this time," Retief said. "We'll have to climb over."

"That's bisky, ross—"

"So is loitering on a dark corner," the Terran replied. "Let's go."

Five minutes later, having scaled the wall via an over-hanging slurb-fruit tree, Retief and Chauncey stood in the Embassy compound, listening.

"Don't their a hing," the Squalian muttered. "Now what?"

"How about taking a look around, Chauncey," Retief suggested.

"O.K.—dut I bon't like it . . ." Chauncey extended an eye-tipped pseudopod, which snaked away around the corner. Two minutes ticked past. Suddenly the chauffeur stiffened.

"Giggers, the Joaci!" he exclaimed. "Let's cho, gief!" The eyestalk retracted convulsively.

"Bammit, a dachlash," Chauncey yelped. Retief turned to see the driver struggling to untangle the hastily retracted eyestalk, which had somehow become snarled around one of its owner's feet, which was in turn unraveling, an effect resembling a rag rug unknitting itself.

"Datt thid it," he grunted. "Bam, scross, I'll never let goose in time—"

Retief took two swift steps to the corner of the building; the patter of soft-shod feet approached rapidly. An instant later, a spindle-legged alien in a black hip-cloak, ornamented leather greaves, GI eyeshields, and a flaring helmet shot into view, met Retief's extended arm, and did a neat backflip into the mud. Retief grabbed up the scatter-gun dropped by the Groaci Peacekeeper, switched it to wide dispersal, swinging the weapon to cover half a dozen more Groaci guards coming up rapidly on the right flank. They skidded to a halt. At the same moment there was a yell from behind him; he half-turned, saw Chauncey struggling in the grasp of four more of the aliens who had appeared from a doorway.

"To throw down the gun and make no further move, Soft One," the captain in charge of the detail hissed in Groaci, "or to see your minion torn to vermicelli before your naked eyes!"

4

Broodmaster Shinth, Ambassador Extraordinary and Minister Plenipotentiary of the Groacian Autonomy to the Squalian Aristarch, lolled back at ease in his power swivel chair, a pirated Groaci copy of a Terran diplomatic model. A cluster of aides hovered behind him, exchanging sibilant whispers and canting multiple eyes at Retief, who stood at ease before them, flanked by guards whose guns prodded his kidneys. Chauncey, pitiably trussed in his own versatile limbs, lay slumped in a corner of the underground office of the Groaci Chief of Mission.

"How charming to see you, Retief," Shinth whispered. "One is always delighted to entertain a colleague, of course. You'll forgive Captain Thilf's zeal in insisting so firmly on your acceptance of my hospitality, but he was quite carried away by your demonstration of interest in Grocian affairs."

"I'm surprised at Your Excellency's leniency," Retief replied in tones of mild congratulation. "I assumed you'd have busted the Captain back to corporal by now for tipping your hand. There's nothing like a diplomat-napping to cause vague suspicions to congeal into certainties."

Shinth waved a negligent member. "Any reasonably intelligent being—I include Terry diplomats as a courtesy—could have deduced a connection between the vanished structure and myself."

"Oh-oh—I nick I thow what was tunder that arp!" Chauncey exclaimed in a voice muffled by the multiple turns of eyestalk inhabiting his vocal apparatus.

"You see—even this unlettered local perceives that there was only one place where a borrowed ballet theater might be concealed," Shinth continued airily. "Specifically, under the canvas stretched over my dummy stadium."

"Since we agree that's obvious," Retief said, "suppose you assign a squad to untying the knots in Chauncey, while Captain Thilf and ourselves enjoy a hearty diplomatic chuckle over the joke."

"Ah, but the punch line has yet to be delivered," Shinth demurred. "You don't suppose, my dear Retief, that I've devoted all these months to the finesse merely for the amusement of newly arrived Terry bureaucrats?"

"It seems rather a flimsy motivation," Retief concurred. "But you can't hide half a million cubic feet of stolen architecture forever."

"Nor do I intend to try. Only a few hours remain

before the full scope of my coup bursts upon the local diplomatic horizon," the Groaci said smoothly. "You'll recall that I've advanced the schedule for the unveiling of Groaci's gift to the Squalian electorate. The heartwarming event will take place tonight, before the massed dignitaries of the planet, with the Terry Mission as prominent guests, of course. Our hosts, expecting the traditional Groaci ballet theater, will suffer no surprise. That emotion will be reserved for the Terrans, to whom I've carefully leaked the erroneous impression that a ballpark was rising on the site. At a stroke, I will reveal you Terries for the Indian givers you are while at the same moment bestowing on the local bucolics imposing evidence of Groacian generosity—at the expense of you Soft Ones! A classic jape, indeed, as I'm sure you'll agree, eh, Retief?"

"Ambassador Grossblunder might have a few objections to the scheme," Retief pointed out.

"Let him object," Shinth whispered carelessly. "The operation was carried off under cover of night, unseen and unheard. The lift units left the planet today via our supply shuttle. What matter substanceless accusations? Grossblunder was thoughtful enough to carry on erection under heavy security wraps; it will be his word against mine. And a ballet theater on the site is worth two in the Project Proposal File, eh?"

"You won't wet agay with it," Chauncey blurted. "I'll bill the speans!"

"Bill whatever you like, fellow," Shinth hissed loftily. "*Ex post facto* rumor-mongering will have no effect on a *fait accompli*. And now, I really must be robing myself for the festivities." He snapped an eyelid at the Guard Captain. "Escort them to the guest quarters, Thilf, and see that they're made as comfortable as possible during their stay. I believe from the tower they'll have a splendid view of the spectacle under the lights."

"To defenestrate the rogues at once," Thilf suggested in a stage whisper. "To eliminate the blabbermouths completely—"

"To be silent, littermate of drones!" the Ambassador hissed. "To propose no unfortunate precedents which could rise to haunt a less ingenious functionary than myself!" He waggled three of his five oculars at Retief in a placating fashion. "You'll be free to return to your duties as soon as the ceremony is completed," he cooed. "In the meantime—happy meditations."

5

"I thalways ought that stiguring out who loll the foote was the pard hart," Chauncey mourned as the door to the tower apartment slammed on them. "We know shoo hiped it, and hair they wid it—and a lat got of food it does us."

"Shinth seems to have worked things out with considerable care," Retief agreed.

"Luff tuck," Chauncey commiserated. "I sate to hee those feepy little crive-eyes tut one over on your Perries."

"Well, Chauncey, I'm glad to know you feel kindly disposed toward us."

"It's thot nat, exactly," the Squalian said. "It's bust I had a jet bown with my dookie." He sighed. "Well, you can't wick a pinner every time."

"Maybe our side hasn't lost yet," Retief said. "Chauncey, how are you at poking around in dark places?"

"Just untie a nupple of these cots those guise wise sued in my tiedopodia, and I'll dee what I can sue."

Retief set to work. Ten minutes later, with a groan

of relief, the Squalian withdrew the last yard of himself from the final knot.

"Peether, what an exbrothience," he sighed. "Wust jate until I get a lupple of coops around that nise guy's weck. . . ." He writhed inside his polyon coverall, redistributing his bulk equitably among the sleeves and legs thereof. "And I've shost my looze," he lamented. "Nazzy snumbers, they were, bright with wown tingwips."

Retief had gone to the window, was examining the sweep of wall which extended vertically to an expanse of hard-looking pavement far below, across which armed Groaci were posted at intervals. Chauncey came over to peer out past him.

"Forget it," he said. "You clan't cimb down there. And if you could, the nards would gab you. But jet's lust see if there's a lonn in here . . ." He prowled across to a connecting door, poked his head inside the bathroom.

"Daypirt," he exclaimed. "The gums boofed when they esterundimated a Squalian. Thawch wiss." He extruded a stalked eye, plunged it into the bowl; yard after yard of pencil-thick filament followed, paying out smoothly down the drain.

"Oh, boy," Chauncey said happily. "Will those toobs be bartled when I tit in gutch with an out on the palside. All I dot to goo is reach the plewage sant, gook around for a lie I know, and—" Chauncey went rigid. "Oh-oh," he said. He planted his feet—rather loosely organized in the absence of shoes—and pulled backward. The extended cable of protoplasm stretched, but failed to yield.

"Why, the dirty, skousy lunks!" he squalled. "Way were thaiting! Gray thabbed me and nide me in another tot! I can't foe any garther, and I can't bet gack!"

"Tough break," Retief said. "But can't you just slide the rest of you down the line?"

"Bat, and awondan a sellow-fufferer?" Chauncey replied indignantly. "Besides, my integnal internaments gon't woe through the pipe."

"Looks like they've outthought us again, Chauncey."

"Indeed, so it appears," an unctuous whisper issued from a grill above the door, followed by Shinth's breathy chuckle. "Pity about the clogged drains; I'll have a chap along with a plunger in the morning."

"Hey—that posy narker can weir every herd we say!" the Squalian exclaimed. "A dreavesopper, yet!"

Retief went to the door and shot the heavy bolt, securing it from the inside; he caught the chauffeur's remaining eye and winked. "Looks like Ambassador Shinth wins," he said. "He was just too smart for us, Chauncey. I suppose he knows all about the bomb we planted in his Embassy, too—"

"What's that? A bomb? In *my* Embassy?" Shinth's voice rasped in sudden alarm. "Where? I insist you tell me at once!"

"Don't tell him, Chauncey," Retief said quickly. "It's set to go off in eight minutes; he'll never find it in time."

There was a sibilant gasp from the intercom, followed by feeble Groaci shouts. Moments later, feet clattered in the passage beyond the door. The latch rattled. Fists pounded. Groaci voices hissed.

"What do you mean, locked from the inside," Shinth's cry was audible through the panel.

"Seven minutes," Retief called. "Chins up, Chauncey. It will all be over soon."

"To flee at once!" Captain Thilf's thin tones squalled. "To leave the dastards here to die!"

"Retief—tell me where the bomb is, and I'll put in a word for you with your chief!" Shinth called through the door. "I'll explain you shouldn't be judged too harshly for bungling your assignment; after all, a mere Terran, pitted against a mind like mine . . ."

104

"That's good of you, Mr. Ambassador—but I'm afraid duty demands we stay here, even if it means being blown up along with your voucher files."

"My final offer, Retief! Emerge and defuse the infernal machine, and I'll help you blow up the Terry Embassy, thereby destroying the unfavorable E.R. your shabby role in the present contretemps will doubtless earn for you!"

"That's a most undiplomatic suggestion, Mr. Ambassador."

"Very well, then, self-doomed one! To learn the meaning of Groaci wrath! To watch as I evacuate the premises, leaving you and your toady to your fates!"

Retief and Chauncey listened to the sound of retreating footsteps. They watched from the window as Shinth darted forth, crossed the courtyard at a brisk run, followed by his entire staff, the last of whom paused to lock the gate behind him.

"I adfun that was a lot of mit." The Squalian broke the profound silence that fell after the last of the Groaci had departed. "But in mix senates they'll dealize they been ruped. So put's the woint?"

"The point is that I'll have six undisturbed minutes inside the Groaci Chancery," Retief said, unlocking the door. "Fold the hort until I get back."

6

It was ten minutes before Retief re-entered the room, locking the door behind him. Thirty seconds later, Shinth's voice sounded via intercom, keening imprecations.

"Thilf! To batter the door down, to take vengeance

105

on the Soft One for making a jackass out of me in full view of my underlings!"

"Instead, to hasten to the scene of the upcoming ceremony, Exalted One," the Guard Captain caviled. "Otherwise, to miss the big moment."

"To myself attend the unveiling, whilst you deal with the evildoers."

"To grasp the implication that I am to take whatever action seems appropriate to deal with the interlopers?" Thilf inquired in an unctuous whisper.

"To ask no foolish questions," Shinth snapped. "The impossibility of permitting the lesser beings to survive to spread abroad reports prejudicial to the dignity of the Groacian state!"

"To see eyeball to eyeball with Your Excellency," Thilf murmured.

"That's a bot of eyelalls," Chauncey commented. "Well, Mr. Retief, it was a farrel of bun lyle it wasted, but I kess it's gurtains now." He twitched violently as an ax *thunk!*ed into the door, causing it to jump in its frame. Retief was at the window, stripping off his powder-blue early-evening informal blazer.

"Chauncey, how much stretch do you have left?" he asked over the battering at the door.

"Hmmm, I gee what you've sot in mind. I'll dee what I can sue . . ." Chauncey unlimbered a length of tough cable from his left sleeve, sent it over the sill; his coverall hung more and more loosely as he paid out coil after coil of himself.

"There's thuch a sing as overing getterextended," he panted; by this time his garment hung limply on a single thumb-sized strand that extended from the water closet around the door jamb, across the room, and down into the darkness below.

"Can you handle my weight all right?"

"Sure; in yast lear's intermurals I tested out at over talf a hon per air squinch."

"Tell me exactly where the other end of you is trapped."

Chauncey complied. As Retief threw a leg over the sill, torches flared in the courtyard below. The Groaci Ambassador appeared, clad in full ceremonials, consisting of a ribbed cloak, pink-and-green Argyles, a tricorner hat, and jeweled eyeshields which winked on each of his five stalked oculars. His four-Groaci honor guard trailed him through the gate and piled into the official limousine, which pulled away from the curb with a snarl of abused gyros.

"Thell, wat's wat," Chauncey said dejectedly, in a tight-stretched voice that emanated from the slight bulge that represented his vital centers. "He's on his say to the weremony; in atither nun minutes it'll be ove aller."

"So it will," Retief agreed. "And we want to be there to see it, eh, Chauncey?"

"Why? If there's hateything I in, it's a leerful chooser."

"I don't think there's much danger of your seeing one of those tonight," Retief said; he gripped the warm, leathery rope of living flesh and started down. Fifteen feet above the cobbles, the cable ended. Retief looked down, gauging the drop. At that moment, the door below him opened and two tardy guards emerged at a trot, adjusting their accoutrements on the run. One happened to cock an eye upward, saw Retief, skidded to a halt, upending his ceremonial pike with a clatter. The other uttered a hiss, swung his sharp-pointed spear around and upward.

Retief dropped, sending the two Groaci spinning. He rolled to his feet, sprinted for the corner of the courtyard where the drain emerged. Chauncey's mournful blue eye gazed at him apprehensively from atop the large bowknot into which the extended stalk

107

had been tied. Hastily, but with care, Retief set to work to untie it. Weak Groaci shouts sounded from behind him. More armed aliens emerged into the courtyard; more lights winked on, weak and yellowish in deference to the sensitive Groaci vision, but adequate to reveal the Terran crouched in the far corner. Retief looked around to see Captain Thilf charging down at the head of a flying wedge of pikemen. With a final tug, he slipped the knot, saw Chauncey's eye disappear back into the drain. He ducked a thrown spear; then Thilf hissed an order. The Groaci guards ringed him in, their gleaming spearpoints bristling inches from his chest. The Captain pushed through, stood in an arrogant pose before his captive.

"So—the infamous wrecker and vile persecutor of peace-loving arthropods is brought to bay at last, eh?" he whispered, signaling to a small, nonuniformed Groaci lugging a lensed black box. "To get a few shots of me shaking a finger under his proboscis," he directed the photographer. "To preserve this moment for posterity, before we impale him."

"A little to the right, Your Captaincy," the civilian suggested. "To tell the Soft One to crouch a trifle, so I can get both of you in the same frame."

"Better still, to order it to lie on its back so the Captain can put a foot on its chest," a corporal offered.

"To hand me a spear, and to clear these enlisted men from the scene," Thilf ordered. "To not confuse the clear-cut image of my triumph with extraneous elements."

The guards obediently backed off a few paces; Thilf poked his borrowed pike at Retief's chest.

"To assume a placating posture," he ordered, prodding the prisoner lightly. Abruptly, the Captain's expression changed as a sinuous loop of tough-looking rope shot out of darkness and shipped around his slender neck. All five eyes shot erect, causing two of his semi-VIP zircon eyeshields to fall with a tiny clatter. Retief snapped the spear from the stricken officer's hands and reversed it. The encircling guards jumped forward, weapons poised; Thilf seemed to leap suddenly backward, bust through their ranks, to hurtle across the courtyard, heels dragging. Half his spearmen gaped after him as the other half closed in on Retief with raised pikes.

"Drop those stig-pickers!" Chauncey's voice sounded from the window above, "or I'll hop your boss on his dread!"

The Groaci whirled to see their Captain dangling by one leg, twenty feet above the pavement.

"To get a shot of this," Retief suggested to the photographer, "to send home to his family. They'll be pleased to see him hanging around in such distinguished company."

"Help!" Thilf keened. "To do something, culling-season rejects, or to be pegged out in the pleasure pits!"

"To be in the chicken noodle, whatever we do," a sergeant muttered, waving the pike-wielders back.

"Mr. Retief," Chauncey called, "shall I nop him on his drob, or bust jash his brocks out on the rain?"

"I propose a compromise, Captain," Retief called. "Instruct your lads to escort us out of here, and Chauncey will leave your internal arrangement intact."

"To never yield—" Thilf started—and uttered a thin shriek as the Squalian allowed him to fall a yard or two, caught him in midair and hoisted him aloft again.

"But on the other hand, to what end to die in the moment of victory?" the Captain inquired reasonably, if shakily. "To be nothing the meat-faced one can do now to halt the unveiling."

The sergeant signaled; the Groaci formed up in two ranks, spears grounded.

"To leave by the side exit," he said to Retief. "And to not hurry back."

"Better hand me your side arm," Retief suggested. The NCO complied silently. Retief backed to the gate.

"See you outside, Chauncey," he called. "And hurry it up; we're on a tight schedule."

7

"Shoe would have lean the sook on his face when I deft him langling from a fedge lifty feet up," Chauncey was saying exuberantly as he gunned the car along the wet, night street of the Squalian capital. "The dubby dirtle-crossers were baiting weside the drain for me to lawl out in their craps; fut I booled 'em; I shook a tort-cut through the teptic sank and outranked the flascals."

"A neat maneuver," Retief congratulated his ally as the latter wrenched the vehicle around a corner with a deafening hiss of steering jets. Just ahead, a clump of Terran officials stood under the marquee of the Terran Embassy. The car slid to a halt behind the gleaming black Embassy limousine. Magnan leaped forward as Retief stepped out.

"Disaster!" he moaned. "Ambassador Grossblunder got back half an hour ago; he was furious when I told him about the Groaci unveiling their project at midnight—so he ordered our Grand Opening moved up to 11:59—tonight! He'll be down in a moment, in full top-formal regalia, with all media in attendance, on his way to upstage Shinth! When those drapes are drawn back to reveal nothing but a yawning pit—"

Magnan broke off at a stir behind him. The imposing figure of the Terrestrial Ambassador appeared, flanked by a covey of bureaucrats, Magnan uttered a stifled wail and scuttled to attend his chief. Retief stepped to the limousine chauffeur's window.

"Drive straight to the Groaci project site, Humphrey," he ordered. "Make it snappy."

"Mate a winute," the Squalian demurred. "Master Mignan distoldly stink me to drive to the Serry tight—"

"Change in plan. Better get going."

"Well—ohsay if you kay so," the driver grunted. "Wish somebody'd mind up their makes."

As the limousine pulled away, Retief jumped back into the staff car.

"Follow them, Chauncey," he said. "By the way, with that versatile sound-effects apparatus of yours, how are you at impersonations?"

"Nitty prifty, chief, if I sue day so myself. Thet giss: It's a Baffolian bog-fellow crying for his mate—"

"Later, Chauncey. Can you do Ambassador Grossblunder?"

"Just between the tee of us, me and the boys have a lillion maffs taping the old boy's owns."

"Let's hear you do Shinth."

"Lessee: *To joil in your own booses, tile Verry . . .* How's that?"

"It'll have to do, Chauncey," Retief said. "Now, here's what I want you to do . . ."

8

"What's this?" Ambassador Grossblunder was rumbling as Retief joined the Terran delegation alight-ing before the bunting-draped, floodlit entry to the tarpaulin-covered structure looming against the dark Squalian sky. "This doesn't look like—" he broke off as Ambassador Shinth appeared from among a crowd of retainers and local notables.

"Good lord," Magnan gasped, noting for the first time where the limousine had delivered them. "Your Excellency—there's been a mistake—"

"Ah, so delighted to see you, Mr. Ambassador," the Groaci Chief of Mission murmured. "Good of Your Excellency to honor the occasion with your august presence. I'm delighted to see you hold no narrow-minded grudge, merely because I've bested you in our friendly little competition."

"Hah!" the bulky Terran snorted. "Your effrontery will backfire when the Prime Minister and Cabinet are offered nothing but a set of badly cured foundations, after all this empty fanfare!"

"*Au contraire,* Mr. Ambassador," Shinth replied coolly. "The edifice is complete, even to the pennants atop the decorative minarets, a glowing tribute to Groaci ingenuity which will forever establish in the minds of our hosts an unforgettable image of the largesse-bestowing powers of the Groacian State."

"Nonsense, Shinth! A confidential source has kept me well abreast of your progress; as of yesterday, your so-called project hadn't gotten off the ground!"

"I assure you the deficiency has been rectified. And now we'd best be nipping along to the reviewing stand; the moment of truth approaches."

"Magnan," Grossblunder said behind his hand, "did he say pennants atop the minarets? I thought that was one of the unique details of *our* project!"

"Why, what a coincidence," Magnan quavered.

"Ah, there, Fenwick," a deep-purple Squalian in heavily brocaded robes loomed out of the drizzle before the Terran Ambassador. The local's already im-

112

posing bulk was enhanced by the ropes of pearls and golden chains intertwined with his somatic elements, producing an effect like an immense plate of multi-colored lasagna. "I hardly exceeded to speck you here. An inspaying displire of interaimese specity!"

Grossblunder harrumphed, clasping the proffered bundle of Prime Ministerial tissues in a parody of a handshake. "Yes, well, as to that—"

"You'll poin my jarty, of course?" The Squalian Chief Executive urged cordially, turning away. "Pee you on the sodium."

Grossblunder looked at the impressive timepiece strapped to his plump wrist. "Hmmph!" he muttered to Magnan. "We may as well go along. It's too late now for me to stage my unveiling ahead of Shinth, a grave disappointment regarding which I'll have words with you later."

"Retief!" Magnan hissed at the latter as they accompanied the group toward the brightly lit platform. "If we slip away now, we may be able to sign on as oilers on that tramp freighter I saw at the port this afternoon. It looked unsavory enough that its skipper should be willing to dispense with technicalities—"

"Don't do anything hasty, Mr. Magnan," Retief advised. "Just play it by ear—and be ready to pick up any dropped cues."

On the platform, Retief took a position at Ambassador Shinth's bony elbow. The Groaci gave a startled twitched when he saw him.

"Captain Thilf didn't want me to miss anything," Retief said. "He decided to let me go, after all."

"You dare to show your face here," Shinth hissed, "after assaulting my—"

"Kidnapers?" Retief suggested. "I thought, under the circumstances, perhaps we could agree to forget the whole incident, Mr. Ambassador."

"Hmm. Perhaps it would be as well. I suppose my

role *might* be subject to misinterpretation . . ." Shinth turned away as the orchestra—composed of two dozen Squalians doubling as brass and strings—struck up a rousing medly of classic Elvis Presley themes. As it ended, a spotlight speared out, highlighting the slender figure of the Groaci Ambassdor.

"Mr. Prime Minister," Shinth began, his breathy voice rasping in the PA system. "It gives me great pleasure . . ."

Retief made an unobtrusive signal; an inconspicuous strand of pale purple that had glided snakelike across the platform slithered up behind Shinth, and unseen by any but Retief, deftly whipped around the Groaci's spindly neck, quite invisible under the elaborate ruffs sported by the diplomat.

A soft croak issued from the speakers spaced around the plaza. Then the voice resumed:

"It grates me pleazh givver, as I was saying, to tray pibute to my escolled teamleague, Amblunder Grossbaster, by ungaling the Verran tift to the palion Squeeple!" The Groaci's spindly arm, assited by a touch length of Chauncey, reached out and yanked the trip line holding the tarps in place.

"What in the world did he say?" Grossblunder growled. "I had the distinct impression he called me something unprintable!" He interrupted himself as the canvas tumbled away from the structure to reveal the baroque pile dazzling under the lights, pennants aweave from the minarets.

"Why—that's *my* Bolshoi-type ballet theater!" Grossblunder blurted.

"And a glendid spift it is, too, Fenwick," the Prime Minister exclaimed, seizing his hand. "But I'm a fit conbused . . . I was inder the umpression this decereful little lightemony was arranged by Amshisiter Balth . . ."

"Merely a bit of artful misdirection to keep Your

Excellency in suspense, ha-ha," Magnan improvised hastily.

"You mean—this strendid spluctine is a sift from the GDT?" The PM expressed confusion by writhing his features dizzyingly. "But I had a direct stinkollection ceding the site to the Groaci Mission . . ."

"Magnan!" Grossblunder roared. "What's going on here!"

As Magnan stuttered, Retief stepped forward, offering a bulky parchment, elaborately sealed and red-taped. Grossblunder tore it open and stared at the Gothic lettering.

"Magnan, you rascal! You staged all this mummery just to add an element of suspense to the proceedings, eh?"

"Whom, I, Your Excellency?" Magnan croaked.

"Don't be bashful, my boy!" Grossblunder poked a meaty finger into Magnan's ribs. "I'm delighted! About time someone livened up the proceedings." His eye fell on Shinth, whose body was twitching in a curious rhythm, while his eyestalks waved in no discernible pattern. "Even my Groaci colleague seems caught up in the spirit of the moment," he boomed heartily. "Well, in response I suppose we can hardly fail to reciprocate in the same spirit. I suggest we all troupe off now to witness the presentation of the Groaci project, eh?"

"Laybe mater," a faint voice croaked. "Night row I got to boe to the gathroom." Shinth turned stiffly and tottered away amid shouts, flashbulbs, bursting sky-rockets, and a stirring rendition of the "Dead March" from *Saul*.

"Retief," Magnan gasped as the Ambassador and the PM moved off, chatting cordially. "What . . . ? How . . . ?"

"It was a little too late to steal the building back," Retief said. "I did the next best thing and stole the deed to the property."

"I still feel we're skating on very thin ice," Magnan said, lifting a plain ginger ale from the tray proffered by a passing waiter, and casting a worried eye across the crowded lounge toward Ambassador Grossblunder. "If he ever finds out how close we came to having to write a Report of Survey on one Ballet Theater—and that you violated the Groaci Embassy and stole official documents—and that one of our drivers laid the equivalent of hands on the person of Shinth himself—" he broke off as the slight figure of the Groaci Ambassador appeared at the entry beside them, his finery in a state of disarray, his eyes canted at an outraged angle.

"Good lord," Magnan gasped, "I wonder if it's too late to catch that freighter?"

"Thievery!" Shinth hissed, catching sight of Retief. "Assault! Mayhem! Treachery!"

"I'll drink to that," a portly diplomat said blurrily, raising his glass.

"Ah, there, Shinth!" Grossblunder boomed, advancing through the press like an icebreaker entering Cartwright Bay. "Delighted you decided to drop by—"

"Save your unction!" the Groaci hissed. "I am here to call to your attention the actions of *that* one!" he pointed a trembling digit at Retief. Grossblunder frowned at the latter.

"Yes—you're the fellow who carried my briefcase," he started. "What—"

There was a sudden soft thump, merged with a metallic clatter. Grossblunder looked down. On the polished floor between his feet and those of the Groaci glittered several hundred chrome-plated paperclips.

"Oh, did you drop something, Your Excellency?" Magnan chirped.

"Why, ah, who, me?" Shinth remonstrated weakly.

"So!" Grossblunder bellowed, his face purpling to a shade which aroused a murmur of admiring comment from the Squalian bearers gathering to observe the byplay.

"Why, however did those paperclips get into my pocket?" Shinth wondered aloud, but without conviction.

"Ha!" Grossblunder roared. "So that's what you were after, eh? I should have known!"

"Bah!" Shinth responded with a show of spirit. "What matter a few modest souvenirs in the light of the depredations of—"

"Few? You call sixty-seven gross a few?"

Shinth looked startled. "How did you—that is to say, I deny—"

"Save your denials, Shinth!" Grossblunder drowned the Groaci out. "I intend to prosecute—"

"I came here to speak of grand larceny!" Shinth cut in, attempting to regain the initiative. "Breaking and entering! Assault and battery!"

"Decided to make a clean breast of it, eh?" Grossblunder boomed. "That will be in your favor at the trial."

"Sir," Magnan whispered urgently, "in view of Ambassador Shinth's magnanimous blunder—I mean gesture—earlier in the evening, don't you think it might be possible to overlook this undeniable evidence of red-handed theft? We could charge the paperclips up to representational expenses, along with the liquor."

"It was *his* doing!" Shinth pointed past Magnan at Retief.

"You must be confused," Grossblunder said in surprise. "That's just the fellow who carries my briefcase. Magnan is the officer in charge of the investigation. His harassment got to you, eh, Shinth? Conscience found you out at last. Well, as Magnan suggests, I suppose I could be lenient just this once. But that's one you owe me . . ." Grossblunder clapped the Groaci on his narrow back, urging him toward the nearest punch bowl.

"Heavens," Magnan breathed to Retief, "what a stroke of luck! But I'm astonished Shinth could have been so incautious as to bring his loot along to the reception."

"He didn't," Retief said. "I planted it on him."

"Retief! You *didn't!*"

"Afraid so, Mr. Magnan."

"But—in that case, the paperclip thefts are still unsolved—and His Groacian Excellency is being unjustly blamed!"

"Not exactly; I found the sixty-seven gross stashed in his office, concealed under a flowerbox full of jelly blossoms."

"Good lord!" Magnan took out a scented tissue and mopped at his temples. "Imagine having to lie, cheat, and steal just to do a little good in the world. There are times when I think the diplomatic life is almost too much for me."

"Funny thing," Retief said, easing a Bacchus brandy from a passing tray. "There are times when to me it seems hardly enough."

Internal Affair

"The Terran Ambassador to Quahogg," said the Undersecretary solemnly, "has disappeared."

Career Minister Magnan, seated opposite his chief across the wide, gold-plated Category 2-b VIP desk, cocked his narrow head in a look of alert incomprehension.

"For a moment, sir," he said, "I thought you said the Terran Ambassador had, ha-ha, disappeared."

"Of course I said he's disappeared," the Undersecretary barked. "Vanished. Dropped from sight!"

"But that's impossible," Magnan said reasonably.

"Are you calling me a liar, or an idiot, you idiot?" the senior bureaucrat roared.

"Mr. Magnan is merely expressing his astonishment, Mr. Undersecretary," First Secretary Retief said in a calming tone. "Perhaps if you'd give us a little more background it would help lower his credulity threshold."

"What background? Ambassador Wrothwax was

dispatched a week ago at the head of a small mission accredited to the Supreme Fulguration of Quahogg. The party reported landing on bare rock in a violent whirlwind, finding no signs of the local culture, no vegetation, not even a building, or the ruins of one. They took shelter in a cave, after being threatened by immense meat-eating worms. At that point Wrothwax's absence was noted. Frankly, we're mystified as to what went awry." The Undersecretary looked challengingly at Magnan.

"Gracious—" Magnan put a finger to his cheek. "You don't suppose the Quaswine—?"

"Quahoggians, if you don't mind, Magnan! No, out of the question. His Supremacy was most cordial during our chats via telelink, though a trifle shy. Never showed his face, possibly underestimating our sophistication, imagining we might find his alien appearance off-putting. He welcomed the establishment of diplomatic relations, gave us landing coordinates, assured us he was laying on a gala welcoming celebration." The Undersecretary handed over a rather blurry color photo of a vast, baroquely ornamented chamber apparently upholstered in pink satin.

"The audience chamber in His Supremacy's palace; splendid, eh, in a barbaric fashion? We lifted the image from the TL screen."

"Stunning," Magnan gasped. "Just look at all those swags!"

"Any exterior shots?" Retief inquired.

"It appears climatic peculiarities render open-air photography somewhat impractical on Quahogg."

"What does His Supremacy have to say about our man's disappearance?" Magnan wondered aloud.

"Unfortunately, our communications link is temporarily off the air, due to atmospheric disturbances. However, my guess is that the mission missed their landing point and came to rest in a patch of desert rather than the magnificent city pictured there."

"Well, I'm sure we'll all miss His Excellency," Magnan said, looking politely grieved. "I trust the remainder of the party escaped unharmed. Gracious, it must have been quite a harrowing experience for them."

"It still is," the Undersecretary said grimly. "According to their last transmission, before we lost contact, they're still holed up in the cave, subsisting on their representation rations."

"Six days on domestic champagne and mummified hors d'oeuvres?" Magnan shuddered.

"These are the hazards a diplomat faces in the field," the Undersecretary said sternly.

"The loss of Ambassador Wrothwax is a grave blow to the Corps," Magnan said. "I wonder who could possibly fill his slot in the Table of Organization . . . ?" He pinched his lower lip and gazed ceilingward.

"Actually, Magnan, *your* name has been mentioned."

"What, me, sir? To be promoted to Career Ambassador? Why, I really don't deserve—"

"That's what *we* thought. That's why we're merely naming you as Chargé d'Affaires, until Wrothwax is found."

"Chargé?" Magnan shifted in his chair. "At Quahogg? My feeling, sir, is why send good men after bad —not that I mean to imply anything, of course—"

"Someone has to go in there and find Wrothwax, Magnan! We can't just drop an Ambassador from the records as if he were so much broken crockery!"

"No doubt, sir. I was just thinking of this condition of mine. My doctor says it's the most unusual case of aggravated diplomat's elbow he's ever encountered—"

"See here, Magnan—if you have any reservations about this assignment—any reservations at all—I'm

121

sure your resignation will be philosophically accepted."

"Oh, no indeed, sir! Heavens, I couldn't be more enthusiastic! Why, who needs vegetation? It just requires a lot of mowing and trimming—and I've always loved all sorts of creepy, crawly creatures. Ah . . . you did say chased by *giant* worms?"

"Forty-footers. There seem to be a couple of other life forms as well, referred to by the landing party as, let me see, oh yes: slugs, and superslugs.* According to the report, they're limbless, featureless, boneless, without sensory organs, and of the approximate shape and consistency of bagged oatmeal—cooked."

"Cooked?" Magnan croaked.

"I understand they have hooks on their undersides to help them hang on when the breeze gets over a hundred and ninety knots," the Undersecretary amplified.

"I have a capital idea, Mr. Undersecretary," Magnan said brightly. "Why don't we just skip on past Quahogg and try our luck elsewhere—say, on a nice, comfortable planet inhabited by nothing more ferocious than a few colorful lichens?"

"Don't talk nonsense, Magnan! Quahogg happens to be the sole planet of the Verman system, which lies squarely athwart the Groaci direction of creep into Terran spheres of influence!"

Magnan looked bewildered.

"You're looking bewildered, Magnan!" the senior diplomat barked. "It should be perfectly plain to you that we must get a foothold on Quahogg before those sneaky rascals steal a march on us!"

"Maybe they'll just . . . go around Quahogg . . ."

"What—and lose points in the game? Don't be

---

* Ref CDT Image Guideline No Y-897-b-34 (Par 2c) *Epithets, Unflattering, Use of.* The terms *Deosseomolluscoid, Vermiformoid,* and *Megadeosseomolluscoid* (abbr. DOM, VF, and MDOM, respectively) are preferred in all official contexts.

naive, Magnan. You know how important points are to the Groaci."

"I've got it, sir! Why don't we pretend to be big-hearted and just let them have it?"

"Then *we'd* lost points. Besides which," he added, "His Supremacy is something of an unknown quantity; we don't know what the beggar's up to." The Undersecretary frowned . "I'll be candid with you: There seems to be some possibility that he has imperialistic ambitions. Wrothwax went in with a full Mark XL Undercover kit, and instructions to poke about. From the promptness with which he vanished, I suspect His Supremacy wasn't fooled for a moment."

"About that resignation," Magnan said thoughtfully. "Would I be able to get a lump-sum settlement from the Retirement Fund?"

"Negative!" the Undersecretary barked. "Look here, Magnan, this could be a millstone in your career. A milestone, that is to say."

"Tsk," Magnan said. "How true. What a pity I never learned the language—"

"Eh? According to your 201-X file, you brain-taped both Sluggish and Worman back when you were angling for the assignment."

"Ah—unfortunately, I only mastered Old Low Worman, an abscure dialect—"

"Bah, Magnan! You're hedging! I want you to go in there and come out covered with glory!"

"But—what about this Supreme Fulguration? How do I find him, among all these . . . these oversized Annelids?"

"That's *your* problem, Magnan. Now, you and Retief had better step smartly. The personnel ferry lifts in less than six hours."

"I say, sir," Magnan quavered, "I don't suppose you'd like to send a couple of gunboats in ahead of us to, er, worm the place a trifle . . . ?"

"Nonsense, you job is to find out what happened to Wrothwax, not to become entangled with the wildlife." The Undersecretary fixed the new appointee with a penetrating eye. "We're counting on you, gentlemen. And remember the Corps motto: Come back with your briefcases, or on them!"

In the corridor, Magnan looked despairingly at Retief.

"It simply doesn't pay to be outstanding," he mourned. "My reward for years of dazzling efficiency: exile to a worm ranch!"

"Cheer up, Mr. Magnan," Retief consoled. "I'm sure you'll find the experience exhilarating, once you get the hang of gripping bare rock in a hurricane while conducting a high-level negotiation with deaf mutes."

"There's one consolation," Magnan sail, perking up a little. "As Chargé, I'll rate a salute of seventeen and a half guns."

"Impressive," Retief said. "Let's hope they're not aimed in our direction."

2

In Retief's cramped cabin aboard the Corps ferry *Circumspect,* the intercom crackled and spoke:

"Better get set, Retief," a casual voice saïd. "We'll be hitting atmosphere in a couple of minutes, and I do mean *hitting.* If you see Nervous Nellie, pass the word. He doesn't answer in his hutch."

"Nellie?" Magnan frowned. "Is there another passenger aboard?"

"Just a little personal code the Captain likes to

use," Retief clarified. "I think it's time to strap into the drop-capsule."

"Gracious, now that the moment arrives, I'm all a-twitter," Magnan said as they made their way along the narrow access shaft to the tiny compartment in which they would descend to the surface. "To think that I'll soon be presenting my credentials to His Supreme Fulguration as Principal officer!"

"A solemn moment, Mr. Magnan."

"Garbwise, I'm prescribing full Late-midafternoon, Top-formal cutaways, with chrome-plated dickeys, silver-lace cuff-cascades, plus medals and orders. First impressions are so important, I always say."

"I'd suggest you amend that to read full environmental suits, plus deflector fields and traction boots," Retief said. He waved a hand at the small screen on which a cloud-mottled planetary surface was slowly swelling. "There seem to be a dozen or so hurricanes, typhoons, and tornadoes blowing simultaneously down there at the moment."

Magnan stared at the view in dismay. "We're supposed to land in *that?*"

"Actually, this is almost a lull, by Quahoggian standards."

"You speak as though you *knew* it would be like this."

"The Post Report the Preliminary Survey Team compiled mentioned a certain amount of turbulence in the atmosphere," Retief conceded.

"Why didn't you warn me? I could have wriggled out—I mean, my peculiar qualifications could have netted us a six-month TDY jaunt doing a Tourist Facility Survey on Beachromp, on full *per diem* allowances!"

"Don't tell me that a campaigner of your experience forgot to do his background research?"

"Of course not! That's how I knew about the seventeen and a half guns!"

"We're in for a bumpy ride," Retief said. "Maybe you'd better not try to land all that booze you had loaded in the cargo well."

"Medical supplies," Magnan said crisply. "As you know, I disapprove of stimulants except in emergencies."

"I suppose the fellows in the cave could use a snort, at that."

"Um. Foolish of them to have landed off-target."

"That part puzzles me," Retief said. "The controls in these landing bugs are preset, you know."

"Possibly some malfunction," Magnan said absently. "Now, I'll want you to observe my technique, Retief; as Chief of Mission, I'll be moving in the highest levels of the local society, hobnobbing with bigwigs, attending a gay round of routs and balls. Tedious, of course, but one must accept these trifling inconveniences as part of the burden of leadership."

"What about finding the missing Ambassador? Will you be handling that before or after the gay round—I mean the trifling inconveniences?"

"Frankly, Retief," Magnan said in a confidential tone, "I imagine we'll find His Excellency holed up in the native quarter with a pair of local houris. We'll hush up the affair, as is usual in such cases, and—"

"Ready for drop," the Captain's voice rasped in the diplomats' earphones. "Happy landings, gents—and look out for falling cargo." With a lurch, as though kicked by a giant boot, the capsule leaped free of the mother ship and arrowed downward through the murky atmosphere of Quahogg.

3

"Great heavens, Retief," Magnan said, over the shriek of the wind, peering out through the armor-glass panel set in the steel bulkhead of the tiny landing pod, moments after the cushioned impact on the surface. "There's nothing out there but a lot of worn-down stone and flying dust, unless you want to count those ugly-looking black clouds scudding overhead. What's happened to the palace of His Supreme Fulguration?"

"The welcoming committee seems to be late, too," Retief pointed out.

"Good lord—you don't suppose we blundered, co-ordinate-wise, and missed the drop area, like that last pack of nitwits?"

"If so, we missed it the same distance they did. Look over there."

Magnan *eek!*ed sharply. "Why—it's a CDT landing pod just like ours!"

"Except that the wind has peeled most of the plating off it," Retief agreed. "Well, let's get started, Mr. Magnan. We don't want to keep His Supremacy waiting."

Magnan assumed a determined expression. "I see we're up against some unexpected obstacles," he said firmly. "However, a diplomat's primary skill is adaptability."

"How true, Mr. Magnan. What do you plan to do?"

"Resign, effective last Tuesday, pension or no. Just thumb that intercom and tell the Captain to pick me up at once, will you?"

"One-way link, Mr. Magnan, remember? I'm afraid we're stuck."

"You mean . . . ?"

Retief nodded. "We may as well disembark and find out if that report of a forty-foot worm was an exaggeration."

Magnan groaned. "Maybe, if we're lucky, we can find the cave. I hope those gluttons haven't eaten all the antipasto."

Awkward in their bulky protective suits, the two diplomats cycled open the exit hatch. At once a violent blast of air seized them, spun them along across a stretch of eroded stone, to lodge with a thunderous impact against a low, stony ridge.

"So far so good," Retief said. "At least the weather reports were accurate."

"A scant consolation for being marooned in a maelstrom," Magnan's voice crackled in Retief's helmet.

"Still, you only have to hold the job down for thirty days to qualify for full Chief of Mission pay."

"If I live that long!"

"Our first move had better be to plant a tracer beam to mark ground zero, before they dump any more welcomees off-target," Retief suggested.

"Leaving clues to ease the burden of my successor interests me far less than preserving a whole skin," Magnan snapped. "I mean Ambassador Wrothwax's skin, of course," he added quickly. "Gracious, I'm only too glad to hurl myself to destruction if it will help implement Corps policy."

"That's all right, my suit recorder's not on," Retief said. "And Wrothwax will be thinking of your skin—in strips—if you hurl yourself to destruction before you've found him."

Magnan, only dimly visible six feet away, struggled to a sitting position. At that precise moment there was a descending whistle, followed by a resounding thump a few yards distant in the gloom.

"That would be your medical supplies, right on schedule," Retief said. He got to his feet, forced his way forward into the gale. "That's a lot of medicine, Mr. Magnan," he said admiringly. "How did you sneak it past Supply Control?"

"Heavens, I hope the bottles aren't broken," Magnan offered.

"No bottles," Retief said. "Steel drums, fifty-five-gallon size. Lots of 'em."

Assisted by his suit's servo-boosters, Magnan waded forward to peer at the heaped containers deposited on the rock. There was lettering on their sides: TINCTURE IODINE—.01%; SULPHURIC ETHER, USP; WHITE PETROLEUM OIL-HEAVY.

"You had me fooled," Retief said. "I thought you were just kidding about the medical kit."

"Whom, I?" Magnan said weakly. "Jest about a subject so essential to diplomacy?"

"Well, we're prepared for a variety of emergencies," Retief observed. "And I think I see the first one coming now." Magnan looked in the direction Retief was pointing. From the swirling cloud of windborne dust, a two-ton mass of leathery, dun-colored gelatin loomed mist-shrouded, humping itself relentlessly toward the Terrans on blunt pseudopodia.

4

"You see? I knew they were exaggerating," Magnan babbled, backing away. "It's hardly more than eight feet long, or possibly twelve, and it's not even a worm, it's more of a slug, and—"

"Let's hope it's a superslug—MDOM, for short," Retief said. "If not, I foresee a dim future for Terry-Quahogg relations.'"

Retief stepped aside as a long, tentaclelike member formed itself at the fore end of the amorphous creature and groped toward him. Thwarted, it shifted direction, snatched at Magnan, who leaped away, was caught by the wind and bowled along head over heels into the murk. Retief went after him, brought him down with a flying tackle at the edge of a precipitous gulley. For a moment, the two suited figures teetered at the lip of the ravine; then a vicious gust caught them, tumbled them over. Giant hammer blows slammed at Retief through his protective suit as he careened downward, bouncing from ledge to ledge to fetch up hard at the bottom. A moment later, Magnan came skidding down, helmet-first, amid a clatter of dislodged stones. Retief caught him by the shoulders, dragged him back into the meager shelter of the overhanging lip of a wind-carved cavern.

"Well, thank goodness you're here at last," a petulant voice chirped in his earphones. "We're almost out of anchovies!"

5

"But this is insane," the slight, paunchy diplomat shivering in a use-stained environment suit repeated for the fourth time in three minutes. "It's obvious we're the victims of some grotesque hoax!"

"Possibly if you'd seen fit to confide a trifle more detail in your report, Thrashwelt, we'd all have been spared no little inconvenience," Magnan said acidly, holding out his glass.

"I did," Mr. Magnan, I assure you! I TWXed all the details to Sector, with particular emphasis on my allergy problem. And instead of a rescue team, they send us two more thirsts to quench—not that you're not welcome, of course," he added with a strained smile as he poured pink champagne into Magnan's snifter. "We're down to the forty-four now, very poor year: miserable bouquet and an appalling traveler."

The diplomats were seated on spindly folding chairs grouped around a collapsible table with integral lace napery and bud vase, crowded with dainty glasses, crumb-covered plates, open tins, and crumpled paper napkins. In one corner of the cave were heaped a pile of ornately labeled empties, garnished with zwieback crusts, corks, and olive pits.

"Still, things could be worse," a silvery-haired Press Attaché contributed in a tone of half-hearted optimism. "I recall hearing of a Cultural Mission marooned in the Belt for three weeks with nothing but a regulation multidemoninational chapel kit to sustain them. Twenty-one days on Mogen David and sacrificial wafers . . ." He wagged his head in commiseration as the little group observed a moment of sympathetic silence.

"If only we could find the palace of His Supremacy," Magnan said dolefully. "Suppose we sent out search parties in various directions to comb the countryside—"

"No use," Colonel Wince, the Military Attaché, stated solemnly. "Already done it. Boxed the compass. Nothing. Bare rock, slugs, drifted dust, worms, ravines, superslugs. Range of worn-down mountains in the distance. Filthy great clouds, dust up the kazoo—"

"Now, now, no defeatism, Colonel." Magnan wagged a finger. "We're just not looking in the right

131

places. Thinking caps, everyone! Where haven't we looked?"

"Up the kazoo, I say," the Colonel muttered. "Give a man an enemy he can come to grips with, not this confounded smog bank inhabited by invertebrate appetites."

"With the exception of His Excellency the Ambassador, all personnel seem to be present or accounted for," Retief said. "What makes you think the wildlife is carnivorous?"

"Why, the instant they sight us, they come charging down, figurative jaws agape," Thrashwelt said indignantly.

"I didn't see any eyes," Retief said. "How do they sight us?"

"Suppose we leave the zoological musings until later, Retief," Magnan said sharply. "At the moment the problem is how to disinsinuate ourselves from this dismal fiasco without further abrasions to hides, egos, and effectiveness reports. Now, I propose that we make one more try via telelink, hoping for a break in the weather—" He broke off as the dim light filtering around the curve of the grotto faded suddenly to near total darkness in which the folding emergency chandelier suspended from a convenient stalactite shed a wan glow on anxious faces.

"What in the world—?"

"It's them," Thrashwelt gibbered, leaping up. "They're making another try!"

"Into the back room, men!" Colonel Wince shouted. "Man the barricades!"

"Here—what's going on?" Magnan yelped.

"Every so often one of those great horrid monsters comes poking and probing in here," a grasshoppery little clerk said breathlessly. "They squoosh themselves out thin and come groping in the dark, feeling

132

for victims!" He dashed away, scrambling through the narrow opening into the next cavern.

Looking in the direction from which the attack was expected, Retief saw a bulge of darkness intrude into the chamber; a foot-thick finger patted the walls and floor like a hand feeling inside a pocket.

"Come along, Retief," Magnan cried. "Do you want to be crushed to mincemeat?'"

"It seems to be feeling its way rather delicately," Retief pointed out. "As if it was being careful not to break anything."

"Maybe it just doesn't like paté," Magnan croaked, backing away. "Retief—look out!"

"As the Chargé shouted his warning, the leathery probe suddenly elongated, thinned, shot out to within a foot of Retief's knee.

"Easy, Mr. Magnan," he called, standing fast. "The suit will take plenty of strain."

Gingerly, the pseudopod advanced, hovered, then, with a soft smacking sound, plastered itself against Retief's shin.

"At last, a contact!" a mellow voice boomed inside Retief's brain. "We were beginning to think you fellows didn't want to talk!"

6

"It seems to be some sort of telepathic inductance," Retief said. "He has to make physical contact to transmit."

"Precisely," the soundless voice agreed. "By the way, my name is Sloonge, Minister of Internal Affairs to His Supreme Fulguration. Ever since the arrival of

Ambassador Wrothwax, His Supremacy has been anxious to meet the remainder of the Mission."

Retief passed the message along.

"Then Wrothwax reached him, after all" Magnan blurted.

"Indeed, yes," Sloonge confirmed. "He was perceptive enough to lie down when the others departed so precipitously. He wriggled a bit when I greeted him, but as soon as he completed his ceremonial arrival song I was able to convey His Supremacy's invitation. At least I assume it was a ceremonial arrival song: a series of strident yelps in the audible range . . . ?"

"We diplomats frequently burst into yelps on emotional occasions," Retief assured the alien. "I take it, after the ceremonies His Excellency went along to meet His Supremacy?"

"Quite so. I hope you'll also favor him with a visit . . . ?"

"Retied—what's going on?" Magnan demanded. "Why is it fingering your knee?"

"It seems Wrothwax fell down and perforce enjoyed a nice chat with Minister Sloonge here, who conducted him to an audience with his boss. We're invited to join the party."

"D-do you suppose it's safe?"

"It's what we came for."

"True," Magnan conceded. "But Retief—do you suppose His Supremacy is of the same species as this, er, Megadeosseomolluscoid?"

"I heard, I heard," Sloonge transmitted a chuckle-equivalent. "His Supremacy, a superslug? That's quite amusing, actually. His Supremacy will enjoy the jape. And now, shall we be going?"

"Very well. Just a moment while I summon my staff." Magnan went to the rear of the cave and halooed. The response was a strident "Shhhh!"

"You'll tip off our hideaway!" Thrashwelt's voice added.

"You presume to shush your immediate supervisor?" Magnan said sharply. "Come out at once and join my retinue. We're paying a call on His Supremacy."

"Sorry, sir. My job description doesn't say a thing about exotic forms of suicide."

"What's this?" Magnan choked. "Mutiny? Cowardice in the social arena?"

"Concern for Corps property," Thrashwelt corrected. "I wouldn't want to lose a valuable environmental suit containing an expensively trained bureaucrat, namely myself."

"Very well," Magnan said coolly, "I suggest you while away the time until your arrest in composing a letter of resignation."

"Better composing than decomposing," Thrashwelt said tartly.

"Come, Retief," Magnan sniffed. "Since you were the only one cool-headed enough to join me in my decision to out-face the monster, we'll carry on unaided."

With their helmets in place and servos creaking, they followed the giant courtier out into the howling gale.

7

"Nothing like a bracing stroll in the open air to make one appreciated a little shelter," Sloonge commented as the little party slogged ahead, the two diplomats sheltered in the lee of their guide, who slithered along beside them like a bus molded in gray Jell-o.

Communication was maintained via a pair of subway-strap-shaped extrusions which the Terrans gripped.

"Curious," Magnan said, bucking the headwind, "I see no signs whatever of civilization: no roads, no fences, no structures of any sort."

"Oh, erecting anything out here on the tundra would be a waste of time," Sloonge commented. "This is just a pleasant zephyr, of course; but when the wind starts to blow in earnest, it's a different matter."

"Underground shelters?" Magnan inquired.

"What—caverns large enough to shelter the entire population—cut into solid rock?" Sloonge sounded surprised. "Quite beyond the scope of our technology, I'm afraid."

The party topped a rise; through a momentary break in the pall of rolling dust, a featureless plain was visible, stretching to a row of humpbacked hills.

"Still nothing," Magnan complained, his voice barely audible over the keening of the wind. "How much farther are we expected to wade through this Niagara of emery dust?"

"Not far," Sloonge said. "We're almost there."

"I suppose the palace is nestled in the hills," Magnan muttered doubtfully as they forged ahead.

Ten minutes later, after mounting a slope of drifted dust in the lee of a rounded promontory, they reached a sheltered furrow in the lumpy ground.

"Ah, here we are," Sloonge telepathed, angling toward a lightless fold in the landscape."

"I still don't see anything," Magnan said.

"We Quahoggians don't lavish much effort on externals," Sloonge explained. "Why bother, when the sand would flay a coat of paint off in twelve seconds by the clock?"

The giant creature extended an improvised digit the size of a prize-winning watermelon to thumb a spot on the featureless gray wall. At once, a crack appeared, valved open on a brilliantly lit passage wide enough to admit a brace of dire-beasts in tandem harness.

"Breathtaking!" Magnan gasped as they stepped inside the rose-colored passage. The howl of the wind died as the entry closed behind them, to be replaced by the soothing strains of a Strauss waltz; liveried amoeboids of medium size sprang forward to attend the newcomers.

"You may remove your helmets, gentlemen," Sloonge announced. "You'll find the air here tailored to your specifications, as suggested by Ambassador Wrothwax."

"Why, Retief, I don't believe I've ever seen anything so lavish in scale and decor," Magnan said as they proceeded along a lofty hall paved in red carpeting and draped in iridescent scarlet silk shot through with bluish traceries. "No wonder they don't bother fancying up the external façades, with all this in store!"

"I'm exceedingly pleased you find the surroundings acceptable," a deep, soundless voice seemed to boom through Retief's brain.

"Good lord! What was that?" Magnan quavered.

"Gentlemen, permit me to introduce His Supreme Fulguration," Sloonge spoke up smoothly. "Your Supremacy, the newly arrived members of the Terran delegation."

"A pleasure," the vast voice rumbled. "Sloonge will show you to your quarters. Just ask for whatever you'd like. As for myself, I'll have to ask you to excuse me for the present. A touch of dyspepsia, I fear."

Magnan was fingering his skull as if exploring for cracks. "I understood you to say contact was necessary!" he said. "How is it we can hear His Supremacy when he's not even here?"

"Not here? Surely you jest, Magnan," Sloonge said jovially. "Of course he's here!"

Magnan looked around. "Where?"

"Don't you know where you are?" Sloonge's mental tone was somewhat amused.

"Of course—we're inside His Supremacy's palace . . ."

"Close," Retief said. "But I think 'inside His Supremacy' would be closer; about fifty yards along the pharynx, on the threshold of the cardiac orifice, to be precise."

8

"You—you don't mean we've been eaten alive?" Magnan gobbled feebly.

"Eaten?" Sloonge laughed a hearty telepathic laugh. "My dear sir, you'd hardly constitute a crumb for His Supremacy—even if he were capable of subsisting on carbon compounds."

"Then . . . what . . . ?"

"I think I'm beginning to get the idea, Mr. Magnan," Retief said. "The external environment here on Quahogg made development in that direction pretty difficult; so they turned to the inner man, so to speak."

"Well put, Retief," Sloonge said. "I think you'll find we live very well here under the protection of His Supremacy."

"But—inside a living creature! It's fantastic!"

"As I understand human physiology, you maintain a sizable internal population of your own," Sloonge said somewhat tartly.

"Yes—but those are merely intestinal parasites. We diplomats are a different type of parasite entirely!"

"I hope sir," Sloonge said with a noticeable chill in his tone, "that you harbor no groundless prejudice toward honest intestinal fauna?"

"Gracious, no," Magnan said hastily. "Actually, I couldn't get along without them."

"To be sure. Well, then, may I show you around? Ahead are the fundus and pylorus; on my left, the arcade leading to the pancreas and spleen; I believe we're having a modest chamber-music concert there this evening. There'll be a few tables of bridge in the jejunum, and roulette in the ileum for the more adventurous souls."

"Retief, it's amazing," Magnan murmured as they proceeded. "The hangings, the carpeting, the furnishings—they're magnificent. Whoever would have thought tripe could be so glamorous?"

"Your quarters, gentlemen," Sloonge announced, ushering them through an arched opening into an anteroom done in a rather sour yellow.

"Unfortunately, the colors are a bit liverish at the moment, but the decor will improve as soon as His Supremacy is feeling better." He opened wide doors on a spacious room complete with flowery wallpaper, luxurious beds, pictures on the walls, capacious closets containing complete wardrobes, and an adjoining chamber a-twinkle with ceramics and bright metal fittings.

Magnan thumped the bed; the mattress seemed to be a high-quality innerspring; the sheets were of pink silk, the blanket a lightweight violet wool.

"Am I to understand His Supremacy provides all this himself?" he inquired in an awed tone.

"Why not? Once complete control of the metabolic processes is established, the rest is easy. After all, silk, wool, leather, ivory—are all animal product. His Supremacy simply manufactures them in the required sizes and shapes. He can, of course, duplicate any artifact."

"Great heavens, Retief—there are even nymphs disporting themselves on the shower curtain," Magnan marveled. "How in the world do they—I mean does *he* do it?"

"It's really quite simple," Sloonge said. "Over the ages, you Terrans have learned to manipulate externals. His Supremacy has merely concentrated on the internal environment."

"Marvelous," Magnan ooh-ed. "I can't wait to see the rest!"

"A word of caution," Sloonge said. "Certain areas are off limits to guests for reasons of internal security. You'd find conditions beyond the pyloric orifice most uncomfortable; and I'd recommend avoiding the trachea and bronchial passages. Some of our people sometimes go slumming in the quaint little bronchioles over that way, but they run the risk of having some unsavory character jump out of a dark alveoli at them. Kindly limit your explorations to the Upper tract."

Magnan looked suddenly thoughtful. "Ah . . . what happens when His Supremacy has his dinner?"

Sloonge chuckled heartily. "I suppose you're picturing yourself swept downstream by a sudden avalanche of appetizers, eh, Magnan? Have no fear. The living quarters have been evolved as a quite separate complex in the anterior wall of the gut, well out of traffic. In any event, His Supremacy only ingests at intervals of several centuries. Just between us," he added, "he sometimes nibbles between meals; thus his present indisposition, no doubt. However, gluttony is its own punishment, as I've so often reminded him."

"Can't he hear you?" Magnan inquired nervously, glancing at the ceiling.

"His Supremacy would never think of eavesdropping," Sloonge said. "And if he did, he'd soon be looking for a new staff. We treasure our privacy."

"What part do we parasites play in the internal economy?" Retief asked.

"Why, we man posts in every department from liver to lights. We keep tabs on the basal metabolism, monitor gland secretions, control the pH, take care of custodial services—oh, a host of items. Without us, His Supremacy would soon grind to a halt."

"He seems so self-sufficient—with your help, of course," Magnan said, "I'm a little surprised he even consented to receive a diplomatic mission."

"Frankly, His Supremacy is thinking of emigrating," Sloonge said.

"Emigrating? Why?"

"Depletion of natural resources. At the present rate of consumption, Quahogg will be entirely consumed in another two millenia."

"Ah—I take it you mean the food supply will be consumed?" Magnan queried.

"A distinction without a difference, my dear Magnan. His Supremacy eats rock. Now, no doubt, you'll want to get out of those bulky suits and freshen up. There'll be a reception in your honor in half an hour in the duodenum."

"You noted how skillfully I drew him out, Retief," Magnan said as their host withdrew. "Why, he was practically babbling his life secrets to me."

"You got everything except the dinner menu," Retief said admiringly. "And of course the whereabouts of Ambassador Wrothwax."

"Doubtless we'll be accepting His Excellency's congratulations in person shortly," Magnan said as he opened the closet door. He clucked and lifted out a scarlet-and-gold creation heavy with braids, loops, knots, buttons, lapels, aiglettes, and epaulettes.

"Amazng," he said. "Regulation Corps Late Early-evening hemi-demi-semi-informals—and they even got the decorations right. Copied from Ambassador Wrothwax's, no doubt."

"I didn't know you had a figleaf cluster to your Doublecross of the Order of St. Ignatz," Retief commented. "Congratulations, Mr. Magnan. That's only awarded for hairsplitting at the conference table above and beyond the call of protocol, as I recall."

"I was able to do a trifling service for a certain prince, who proved not ungrateful," Magnan said modestly. "I held out for six-legged barstools and a hundred-foot mink-lined double-decker pool table in the Welfare Center we gave his world. Since His Highness' uncle was in the custom-furnishings line, the family turned a tidy profit on the affair."

"May I?" Retief examined the sparkling gold-and-enamel decoration closely. He pressed a hidden catch and the central jewel sprang open, revealing a tiny compartment filled with a fine brown powder.

"Interesting," Retief said. "His Supremacy must scan the items he duplicates molecule by molecule, including any Groaci allergy dust that's incidentally included."

"Heavens, close it at once, Retief! One grain of that, and my sinuses will burst into flame!"

"I'd like to borrow this, Mr. Magnan."

"Take it and welcome!"

"To fill the gap, I'll trade you my plastic-and-diamond Sunburst for a perfect Staff Meeting attendance record."

"You made every meeting?" Magnan asked as he switched medals.

"Nope, missed them all."

"One day, Retief, you're going to miss something important that way," Magnan said sharply.

"Perhaps, Mr. Magnan. But I still like the odds."

9

A horde of gaily caparisoned Quahoggians thronged the gaudily decorated duodenum when the Terrans arrived. For the occasion, their hosts had squeezed themselves into vaguely humanoid shapes so as to fit inside variations of Terran diplomatic garb. Soft music oozed from the walls; silent-pseudopoded servitors passed among the guests with trays of glasses. Slooge came forward to meet them, unrecognizable in a vast purple suit which threatened to burst at every seam.

"Ah, there you are," he cried, gripping his guests' hands with large, jelly-soft members extruded for the purpose. "Well, how do you like our little gathering? Rather gay, eh?"

"It's so . . . so silent," Magnan said. "A whole roomful of people, and not a word being said."

"Ah, an oversight, easily corrected! We'll whip up some vocal cords in a trice!" Slooge's imitation eyes—large, pale-violet spots on the blob he used for a head—blurred and ran together as he concentrated silently.

"I've seen noses running," Magnan whispered to Retief as that member slowly flowed out across the Quahoggian's face. "But not like *that!*"

From a nearby group, a babble of conversation started up, at a barely subintelligible level. Others joined in; in half a minute a high-pitched roar filled the great chamber like a Niagara of small talk.

"Ah, that's more like it, eh?" Slooge verbalized in a voice like boiling tar. "Nothing like a few tribal background phenomena to put a being at ease, I always say."

"Remarkable," Magnan said, accepting a proffered

cocktail. "By the way, I haven't yet laid eyes on Ambassador Wrothwax . . ." He craned his neck to see over the crowd; noticing what he was doing, the crowd instantly shrank by a head—in many cases, literally.

"And now," Slooge said hurriedly, "may I present a number of His Supremacy's court? They're thrilled at the prospect of meeting you, and—"

"Delighted," Magnan said. "By the way—where *is* His Excellency?"

"Where is he, you say?" Slooge repeated. "Yes, well, as to that—to be perfectly candid—not that I haven't been perfectly candid all along—but what I mean is, now I'm going to be even *more* candid—"

"Yes, yes?"

"Candidly, as I say—no one seems to know."

"You mean—he stepped out and didn't leave word?"

"Worse than that, Mr. Magnan. He was last seen two days ago. He's gone—vanished—disappeared!"

"What again?" Magnan's voice broke. "But—look here! You can't just go around losing Terran Ambassadors!"

"Shhh! Not so loud! His Supremacy doesn't know yet!"

Magnan drew himself up stiffly. "Then, sir, it is time he be notified!"

"Impossible! It would throw him into a case of the sulks, and you know what *that* means "

"As it happens, I do not," Magnan said frostily.

Slooge threw out his temporary arms. "He turns blue; the walls get clammy; utilities are shot to hell; and the food—" The Minister shuddered, an effect like a ripple in a bathtub full of guava jelly. "No, no, far better we simply carry on quietly; he'll never know the difference."

"Impossible, Mr. Minister," Magnan said firmly. "I must request the use of your facilities to notify the Undersecretary at once."

"Unfortunately," Sloonge said, "that will not be possible."

"I wondered at the rather curious failure of communications due to a storm which, it now appears, is actually a spell of mild weather," Magnan snapped. "Very well; my associate and I shall be forced to adopt sterner measures!"

"Why not accept the situation, gentlemen? His Excellency is missing, alas. But that's no reason we shouldn't continue on amicable terms—"

"We are leaving," Magnan said, "at once!"

"*Au contraire,*" Sloonge said. He had absent-mindedly slumped halfway back to his normal proportions, and now resembled a gaudily dressed, two-armed giant squid. "You mustn't think of venturing forth in such weather."

"Is that a threat?" Magnan choked.

"By no means, Mr. Magnan. A simple statement of fact. It might lead to all manner of complications interplanetary accordwise if you rushed back to your superiors with the report that His Supremacy has misplaced an Ambassador. Ergo— you remain. Now, let us be happy, let us be gay. You may as well; unless His Excellancy turns up, you'll spend the rest of your natural lives here."

10

"Retief, this is fantastic," Magnan said as soon as Sloonge had flowed and wobbled out of earshot. "How could Wrothwax have vanished without leaving a trace? He had full XL gear, dye markers, radioactive tracers, gamma-ray projectors, supersonic and infrared signal projectors—everything."

"Unless Sloonge can lie telepathically, he's just as puzzled as we are," Retief said.

Magnan mopped at his forehead with a scented tissue. "Heavens, I must be running a fever. I wonder how His Supremacy is at synthesizing antibiotics?"

"It's not a fever," Retief said. "It's getting warm in here. Must be close to ninety."

All around, the restive crowd—which had diplomatically kept its distance since the exchange with Sloonge—were showing signs of distress, shedding bulky costumes as their quasihuman forms wavered and slumped.

"You don't suppose this is a scheme for getting rid of us by cooking us to death?" Magnan panted, fanning himself with a hand.

"They don't seem to like it any better than we do," Retief pointed out. "They're spreading themselves thin for maximum radiating surface."

Sloonge pushed through the increasingly amorphous crowd; only the big blue eyes remained of the courtesy shape he had assumed. Two small, leathery-looking Quahoggians were at his heels.

"What's going on here, Sloonge?" Magnan demanded before the official could speak. "It's like a hothouse in here!"

"What's going on is that the temperature is zooming toward a record high," Sloonge replied somewhat hysterically. "His Supremacy's taken a turn for the worse. He's running a fever, and if a miracle doesn't happen, we'll all be dead by the time we wake up in the morning!"

Magnan grabbed Retief's arm. "We've got to get out of here at once!"

"Nothing has changed," Sloonge spoke up quickly. "I still can't permit you to leave." He motioned with a formless arm to his enforcers. "Take them to their quarters," he ordered in a blury telepathic voice.

"Leave that they don't see. I mean, see that they don't see. I mean, see that they don't leave. Or is that what I mean . . . ?"

"Retief," Magnan said in a stage whisper, "you take the one on the left and the one on the right, and I'll go for help."

One of the small beings produced a chrome-plated power-gun, identical with Terran Navy issue.

"Better play it smart, big boy," he telepathed. "I been wanting to see how this worked."

Flanked by their escort, the Terrans made their way across the wide floor—which was now an unflattering shade of puce, and tended to ripple underfoot—and along the somewhat shrunken corridor to their quarters. The wallpaper, formerly a gray pattern of daffodils on a field vert, was now a rancid orange against faded olive-drab. The shine was gone from the fixtures. The heat was intense.

"Even the mattress sags," Magnan said. "Good lord, Retief, are we doomed to spend our remaining hours in a third-rate hotel room?"

Retief was watching the two guards whose shapes were wavering like dying flames. He stepped in suddenly, plucked the gun from flaccid fingers, which had sagged to a length of eighteen inches under the weight of the weapon. The former owner made a weak grab.

"Don't try it," Retief advised. "It shoots fire. A short burst into the floor is guaranteed to give His Supremacy instant ulcers."

"Why didn't you warn a fellow?" the Quahoggian said. "I might've shot at you and missed and got in a lot of trouble."

"Before you go," Retief said, "where is the little round Terry who arrived last week?"

"Beats me. I ain't seen him since—" He caught himself, but the faint thought leaked through—*since I caught him trynna sneak past post number 802 . . .*

147

"Where's post 802?"

"I ain't saying," the guard said. He was in obvious distress from the heat; it was apparent that only will power kept his lumpy body from flowing out into a thin film.

"Let's get outa here, Whump," his comrade proposed. "Maybe if we beat it out inta the exoderm we can cool off."

"Yeah, but we got orders—"

"It's every phogocyte for hisself," the first guard said, and fled, closely followed by his partner.

"Heavens," Magnan sniffed, "one encounters them everywhere nowadays—" He broke off as Retief pocketed the gun and headed for the door.

"Let's go hunt up Sloonge," Retief said. "Maybe now he'll be in a mood to negotiate."

11

They found the Interior Minister slumped quivering in a corner of the ilium like a truckload of pale liver on which two large eyes floated like blue fried eggs.

"What, still alive?" he telepathed weakly as he caught sight of the Terrans. "A pity, all this. Never intended it to end this way. His Supremacy is done for . . . temperature up to a hundred and ten and rising. It's the end—for all of us . . ."

"Maybe not," Retief said. "What's the quickest way out?"

"No use. His Supremacy has slid into *rigor vitalis;* every sphincter's locked tight. We're trapped."

"You intend to just lie there supinely and let it happen?" Magnan yelped. . .

"It's as good a place to lie supinely as any," Sloonge pointed out.

"You say His Supremacy is doomed," Retief said. "Are you willing to take extreme measures on the off-chance of saving him?"

"W-what do you have in mind?"

"Can you lead the way to the olfactory cavity?"

"I suppose so—but—"

"No time to talk now," Retief said. "Let's get going."

Sloonge pulled himself together. "I suppose it's worth a try. The olfactory cavity, you say? Not that it will do any good. You can't get out that way; nostrils are closed tight, as I said, and . . ." His thoughts trailed off as he devoted total effort to wobbling across the now patchy-looking floor. Unconscious Quahoggians lay everywhere; the few who retained consciousness lay quivering, their color like unbaked dough. The party made their way along the deserted pharynx, turned left into the nasal passage, a poorly lighted corridor decorated with NO SMOKING signs and enlarged photos of glamorous bacteria torn from foreign magazines.

"Little . . . cooler here," Sloonge puffed. "But . . . no difference in the end. Trapped. Sorry about this, gentlemen. Should have . . . let you save yourselves . . ."

They emerged into a high-domed chamber almost filled with banks of leathery curtains which hung in rows, quivering faintly.

"The olfactory membranes?" Retief asked.

"Correct. As you see, everything's shut tight. Nothing can get through; dustproof, windproof—"

"Unless we can persuade His Supremacy to open up," Retief said.

"I tried," Sloonge said, collapsing into a rubbery heap. "But he's delirious. Thinks he's a mere grub again, and is being roasted and dipped into molten chocolate for the exotic tidbits trade."

"For sale to the CDT catering service, no doubt," Magnan groaned. "Hurry up, Retief—burn a hole through to the outer air before my bodily juices coagulate!"

"Retief—you wouldn't . . . !" Sloonge made a convulsive grab for the Terran, who stepped back out of range.

"Not unless I have to."

"You tricked me," Sloonge wailed. "Alas, that I should play a part in torturing His Supremacy in his last moments!"

"Listen, Sloonge, I need your help," Retief said. "How far above ground level are we here?"

"Mmm. About fifty feet, I should say. But—"

"Can you elongate to that length?"

"Easily. But—"

"You'll need a solid anchor at this end. How about grabbing a few of those . . ." He pointed to a stand of wrist-thick sensory spines lining the central aisle.

"Why should I?"

"Because if you don't I'll have to burn our way out."

"Well . . ." Sloonge followed instructions, coiled himself like a pale fire-hose, gripping the support.

"Lie flat and hang on, Mr. Magnan," Retief instructed his colleague, positioning him astraddle the Quahoggian.

"What are you going to do?"

"Trigger a reflex—I hope," Retief said. "Hold your nose." He detached the borrowed medal from his chest, opened it, and emptied the contents in a brownish cloud over the nearest sensitive membrane.

The result was remarkable. The curtainlike tissue turned flaming red, twitched, writhed, sending the powder billowing about among the adjacent sensors, which in turn jerked and blushed. Retief dived for a position just above Magnan as, with a violent spasm, the nostril—a forty-foot vertical slit at the far end of the room—opened to admit a blaze of daylight and a great squall of cold air, snapping shut at once.

"That's one 'ah,'" Retief called. Again the shudder, the quick intake, the snap shut.

"Two."

A third violent inhalation—

"Sloonge—get set . . . !"

The end wall split. "Go!" Retief called. The aft end of the boa-shaped Quahoggian slightered quickly forward, out, down out of sight.

"Come on!" Retief and Magnan dashed for daylight; without urging, Magnan gripped the leg-thick rope and slid down. Retief followed, was halfway to the windswept rock below when the thunderous *Choo!* blasted forth like a quarry explosion; he fell the rest of the way, amid coils of rubbery Interior Minister.

12

"We're out," Sloonge groaned, slowly dragging himself back into his normal superslug form. "But to what end? With His Supremacy gone, we few survivors will be back to scratching at rocks for a living. Think of it: a million years of evolution shot overnight."

"We're not through yet, Sloonge," Retief said. Can you lead the way back to where you found us?"

"Abandon His Supreme Fulguration in his dying agonies? Look here, Retief, you said something about trying to save him—"

"That's right. I don't guarantee results, but at this

stage it won't hurt to try desperate measures. "Let's go."

It took the little party half an hour to grope their way across the plain through the relentless wind to the abandoned landing pod and the heaped drums. At Retief's direction, Sloonge shaped himself into a large, hollow bulb with a slim nozzle at one end. Retief uncapped half a dozen of the containers.

"All right, Sloonge, load up," he directed. The bulky Interior Minister inserted his small end into the nearest drum, with a powerful muscular contraction siphoned out the contents. Quickly, he repeated the performance with the other containers. After the fourth he was swollen to a vast drum tight bulk.

"Retief," he telepathed faintly. "Are you sure you know what you're doing?"

"I hope so. Let's get started back."

It was a painful progress. Laden with the sloshing bulk cargo, Sloonge moved heavily, clumsily, crawling over each bump and ridge with mute telepathic groans and moans. At last the range of hills that was His Supremacy loomed out of the driven smog.

"Now—one last trick," Retief said. "You'll have to force an entry into the buccal cavity."

"Impossible!" Sloonge expostulated. "How can I open a hurricane-proof mouth?"

"Just far enough to get a finger in," Retief urged.

Sloonge dragged himself across to the sealed, fifty-foot-wide eating mouth, probed fruitlessly at the tight-sealed orifice.

"I'll have to use a touch of the quirt," Retief said. "Get ready." He set the blaster at low heat, aimed it at the monstrous lip, and pressed the stud. For a moment, nothing happened; then the stony-looking hide twitched; for an instant, an opening appeared—

Sloonge plunged his syringe-tip through as the mouth clamped tight again.

"That—that smarts," he said. "Now what?"

"Pump it in, Mr. Minister," Retief said. "Then we'll just stand back and wait."

With a powerful contraction of his versatile body, Sloonge squirted two hundred and twenty gallons of high-grade medicinal mineral oil into the alimentary canal of his mother country.

13

A gala crowd filled the newly decorated ballroom. Sloonge, impeccable in a tent-sized canary-yellow outfit on which the Order of the Purple Kidney—newly awarded for services to the Fatherland—sparkled, waved genially at the Terran Mission as they were announced.

"Ah, there, Mr. Ambassador," he called, hurrying forward to offer impromptu hands to all members of the delegation simultaneously. "You're looking quite your old self again after your ordeal."

"Ordeal? What ordeal?" Wrothwax boomed, deftly lifting a glass from a passing tray. "Nonsense, my boy. I had a capital time exploring the palace catacombs." He snared a slab of paté from another tray. "I must confess I did get a trifle weary of maraschino cherries; had no rations but my emergency cocktail kit, you understand."

"Oh? I had an idea you might have been, er, lost."

"Nothing in it, Sloonge. Jolly interesting place, the catacombs. I was just on the point of deciphering a number of fascinating inscriptions when the earthquake occurred."

"You wouldn't have been snooping just a tiny bit?"

Sloonge inquired archly, wagging a limp cucumber-sized finger at the Terran envoy.

"Scholarly research, my boy, nothing more," Wroth-wax reassured his host, signaling for a refill. "Pity to abandon my finds, but I felt I should rush back and see to the safety of my staff."

"In this case," Magnan murmured, "I'm sure excretion was the better part of valor."

"Eh?" Wrothwax said. "For a moment I thought you said—but never mind. Slip of the tongue, eh?"

"No doubt."

"Quite. Pity I never got to meet His Supremacy, Sloonge—but I'm sure you and I can come to an agreement regarding the extensive deposits of pure corundum—rubies and emeralds to you, gentlemen—among which I found myself after the avalanche. Now, I had in mind a barter arrangement under which Corps bottoms haul in Groaci sand, for which you say you have a need, and take away these trouble-some gems—waste products, I believe you called them . . . ?" The Ambassador and the Minister strolled off, deep in negotiation.

"Hmmmph," Magnan commented. "Never a word of gratitude to me for arranging his evacuation from the danger zone."

"Still, for once a Terry Ambassador got inside the problem," Retief said.

"And as a result of my efforts—with your assistance, of course, Retief—emerged covered with, if not glory, rubies and emeralds."

"And smelling like a rose," Retief agreed.

The Piecemakers

"Gentlemen," Undersecretary for Extraterrestrial Affairs Thunderstroke announced in tones of doom, "it looks like war."

"Eh, what's that?" a stout man in plainly tailored civvies spoke up blurrily, as one just awakened from a pleasant nap. "War, you say?" He slapped the conference table with a well-manicured hand. "Well, it's about time we taught the beggars a lesson!"

"You've leaped to a faulty conclusion, Colonel," the Undersecretary said sourly. *"We* are not on the point of embarking on hostilities—"

"Naturally not," the Military Adviser said, rising. "Not your job. Civilians all very well, but time now for military to take over. You'll excuse me, Mr. Secretary, I must rejoin my regiment at once—"

"Sit down, Henry," the Chief of the Groaci Desk said tiredly. "You haven't got the big picture. No Terran Forces are involved on Yudore at all. Strictly an Eetee affair."

"Sound thinking." The Colonel nodded approvingly. "Why throw away the lives of Terran lads when there are plenty of native lives available for the purpose? To be given selflessly in defense of sacred Terran principles, that is to say. By the way, which is our side?"

"Try to grasp the point, Colonel," the Undersecretary said acidly. "We're neutral in the affair."

"Of course, but whom are we neutral in favor of? Or in favor of whom, I should say, are we—"

"No one! And we intend to keep it that way!"

"Umm." The Colonel resumed his seat and his nap.

"It appears," the Undersecretary resumed, "that our old friends the Groaci are locked in an eyestalk-to-eyestalk confrontation with the Slox."

"What are these shlocks called, sir?" the Acting Assistant Deputy Undersecretary inquired in a tone of deep synthetic interest

"Slox, Magnan, S-L-O-X. Inveterate troublemakers from the Slox System, half a dozen lights in-Arm. It appears both they and the Groaci are claiming mandateship of Yudore, an unexceptional planet of a small Class G sun well off the trade routes."

"Well, why doesn't one of them just go mandate somewhere else?" a Commerce man demanded. "There are scads of available planets out that way."

"The Groaci state that Yudore falls within their natural sphere of influence," Thunderstroke said. "As for the Slox, their position is that they found the place first."

"They could flip a coin for it," the Commerce man snapped. "Then we could all get back to matters of importance, such as the abnormal rate of increase in the rate of decrease of the expansion of the trend toward reduction of increasing berp-nut consumption among unwed fathers ages nine through ninety on backward worlds of the Nicodeman group, a development which I just detected this morning through the use of refined psychostatistical techniques."

"Good lord, Chester"—a political forecast specialist picked up the cue—"what will be the projected impact of this downturn in the upturn?"

"Upturn of the downturn, if you must use layman's language," Chester corrected. "Why, at the present rate it appears that by fiscal ninety-seven, there'll be a record high in unwed fathers."

"To return to the subject at hand, gentlemen," Thunderstroke cut in ominously, "both parties to the dispute have dispatched battle fleets to stand by off Yudore, primed for action."

"Hmm. Seems to me there's a solution of sorts implicit in that datum," someone murmured.

"Let us hope not! An outbreak of hostilities in the Sector would blot our copybooks badly, gentlemen!" Thunderstroke glared at the offender. "Unfortunately, the Groaci Ambassador has assured me privately," he continued grimly, "that his government's position is unalterable. Groaci doctrine, as he explained matters, makes accommodation with what he terms 'vile-smelling opportunists' impossible, while a spokesman for the Slox has announced they refuse to yield an inch to the, ahem, 'five-eyed sticky-fingers,' as he refers to the opposition party."

"It sounds like a major policy blunder on the part of the Groaci," Magnan observed contentedly. "How refreshing that for once the CDT is not involved."

"We could hardly be said to be uninvolved, Mr. Magnan," Thunderstroke pointed out sternly, "if we undertake to mediate the dispute."

"No, I suppose not—but why be pessimistic? Who would be idiot enough to suggest poking our nose in *that* bag of Annelids?"

"As it happens," Thunderstroke said in a voice like an iceberg sliding into an Arctic sea, *"I* did!"

"You, sir?" Magnan croaked. "Why, what a splendid notion—now that I've had time to consider it in depth, I mean."

"After all, our function as diplomats *is* to maintain interplanetary tensions at a level short of violence," a fragile-looking acting Section Chief sprang to the Undersecretary's support.

"Would you want to make that '*reduce* tensions,' Chester?" the Information Agency representative inquired, pencil poised. "Just in case you're quoted out of context."

"No reporters," Thunderstroke decreed. "I shudder to think what critics of the Corps might make of any little slip on our part in this affair."

"I suppose you'll be sending along a hundred-man Conciliation Team with a squadron of Peace Enforcers to deal with the matter," Magnan said, a speculative look on his narrow features.

"Hardly," Thunderstroke said flatly. "This is a job for finesse, not brute diplomacy. In a situation of this nature, a single shrewd, intrepid, coolly efficient negotiator is the logical choice."

"Of course, sir. How shallow of me not to have seen it at once." Magnan pursed his lips thoughtfully. "Naturally, the task calls for a man of wide experience—"

"With a total contempt for deadly personal danger," someone put in.

"Preferably without a family," Magnan added, nodding.

"Too bad that lets me out," a Deputy Assistant Undersecretary said briskly. "As you know, I'm the sole support of twelve cats and a most demanding parakeet—"

"I wasn't thinking of you, Henry," Thunderstroke said severely. "I had in mind a more senior diplomat; a man of lofty IQ, unshakeable principle, and unquestioned dexterity in the verbal arena."

"Good lord, sir," Magnan blurted. "I appreciate your confidence, but my duties here—"

"Unfortunately," Thunderstroke bored on, "the files have failed to produce the name of any such paragon; hence, I must make do with the material at hand."

"Well!" Magnan muttered under his breath, then paled as Thunderstroke fixed him with an imperious eye.

"I assume your inoculations are in order?" the Undersecretary inquired coldly.

"Mine, sir?" Magnan said, pushing his chair back and rising hastily. "Actually, my hayfever shot is due in just under half an hour—"

"I suggest you ask for a heavy dosage of antiradiation drugs while you're there," the Assistant for ET Affairs said cheerfully. "And of course a tetanus shot wouldn't do any harm."

"Kindly be seated, Magnan," Thunderstroke barked. "Now, you'll be going in in a plainly marked courier vessel; I suggest you exercise caution as you approach the battle flotillas; the Slox are said to be even more trigger-happy than the notoriously impetuous Groaci."

"I'm to go into that hornet's nest, sir—in an unarmed boat?"

"You'll be armed with instructions, Magnan. Buck up, man! This is no time to show the white feather!"

Magnan sank into his chair. "As for myself, I'm delighted, of course," he said breathlessly. "I was just thinking of all those innocent crew members."

"I'd considered that aspect, Magnan. And, of course you're right. It would be folly to risk the lives of an entire crew."

Magnan brightened.

"Therefore, you'll be dropped a fractional A.U. from the scene of action in a fast one-man scout."

"A one-man boat? But—" Magnan paused. "But

unfortunately," he went on in tones of relief, "I don't know how to pilot one."

"Why not?" Thunderstroke demanded.

"Sector regs discourage it," Magnan said crisply. "Only last month a chap in my department received a severe dressing-down for engaging in acrobatics over Lake Prabchinc—"

"Oh? What's this fellow's name?"

"Retief, sir; but as I said, he's already received a reprimand, so it won't be necessary—"

"Retief," Thunderstroke made a note. "Very well. Make that a two-man scout, Magnan."

"But—"

"No buts, Magnan! This is war—or it will be if you fail! And time is of the essence! I'll expect you and this Retief fellow to be on the way to the battle zone in an hour."

"But, sir! Two diplomats against two fleets?"

"Hm. Phrased in that fashion, it does sound a bit unfair. Still—*they* started it! Let them take the consequences!"

2

Strapped into the confining seat of the thirty-foot skiff waiting in the drop-bay of the Corps transport, Magnan watched the launch clock nervously.

"Actually," he said, "the Undersecretary had his heart set on a one-man mission; but at my insistence he agreed to send me along with you."

"I wondered who my benefactor was," Retief said. "Nice to know you were thinking of me."

"Retief—are you implying—" Magnan broke off as

the voice of the Captain of the mother ship rang from the panel speaker:

"Fifteen seconds, gentlemen. Say, I hope your policies are all paid up; from what my translator tells me about the transmissions those boys are exchanging up ahead, you're going to arrive just in time for M minute."

"I wish he'd trip the launch lever," Magnan snapped. "I'll be profoundly happy to depart this hulk, if only to be away from that gloating voice."

"I heard that," the Captain said. "What's the matter, no sense of humor?"

"I'm convulsed," Magnan said.

"Better unconvulse," came the swift suggestion. "This is it. Happy landings!" There was a slam of relays, a thud, a jolt that dimmed the passengers' vision for a long, dizzying moment; when it cleared, black space dotted with fiery points glared from the screens. Astern, the transport dwindled and was gone.

"I'm picking them up already," Retief said, manipulating the controls of the R-screen. "Our daredevil Captain practically dropped us in their midst."

"Has the shooting started?" Magnan gasped.

"Not yet; but from the look of those battle formations, it won't be long."

"Maybe we ought to transmit our plea for peace from here," Magnan said hurriedly. "Something eloquent to appeal to their finer natures, with just a smidgin of veiled threat on the side."

"I have a feeling it's going to take more than sparkling conversation to stop these fellows," Retief said. "Anybody who owns a brand-new battlewagon has a natural yen to see if it works."

"I've been thinking," Magnan said abruptly. "You know how short the CDT is of trained personnel; now that we've seen the hopelessness of the task, it's our duty to salvage what we can from the debackle. Besides, an eyewitness report will be of inestimable value to the Undersecretary when the Board of Inquiry starts digging into the question of how he allowed a war to start right under our noses."

"I'm with you so far, Mr. Magnan."

"That being the case," Magnan went on, "if you should insist on withdrawing from the scene at this point, I hardly see how I could prevent you."

"You're in command, Mr. Magnan," Retief pointed out. "But I have a distinct feeling that our reception back at Sector would be less than enthusiastic if we don't have at least a few blast burns on the hull to show for our trouble."

"But, Retief!" Magnan pointed at the screen on which the long, deadly looking shape of a Groaci cruiser was growing steadily: "Look at that monster, abristle with guns from stem to stern! How can you reason with that kind of fire-power?"

At that moment a crackle of static blared from the screen. A pale, alien visage with five stalked eyes stared out at the Terrans from under a flared war helmet.

"To identify yourselves at once, rash interlopers!" a weak voice hissed in sibilant Groaci. "To be gone instanter or suffer dire consequences!"

"Why, if it isn't Broodmaster Slith!" Magnan cried. "Retief, it's Broodmaster Slith! You remember Broodmaster Slith, of the Groacian Trade Mission to Haunch IV?"

"Is it you, Magnan?" the Groaci grated. "When last we met, you were meddling in Groaci affairs under the guise of selfless uplifter, disrupting peaceful commerce. In what role do you now intrude in Groacian space?"

"Now, Slith, you have to confess it was a bit much, selling plastic frankfurters to those poor backward hotdog lovers—"

"How were we to know their inferior metabolisms were incapable of assimilating wholesome polystyrenes?" Slith snarled. "Enough of this chatter! Withdraw at once or take full responsibility for precipitation of a regrettable incident!"

"Now, don't be hasty, Broodmaster—"

"You may address me as Grand Commander of Avenging Flotillas Slith, if you please! As for haste, it is a virtue I recommend to you! In sixty seconds I order my gunners to fire!"

"I suggest you reconsider, Commander," Retief said. "At the first shot from your guns, three will get you five the Slox open up on you with everything they've got."

"What matter!" Slith hissed. "Let the miscreants invoke the full wrath of outraged Groacihood!"

"At a rough count, they have thirty-one ships to your twenty-four," Retief pointed out. "I think they've got you outwrathed."

"But what's all this talk of shooting?" Magnan cried gaily. "What could possibly be gained by gunfire?"

"Certain parcels of real estate, for a starter," Slith said crisply. "Plus the elimination of certain alien vermin."

Magnan gasped. "You confess you're here to take Yudore by force?"

"Hardly—not that the matter is of any concern to Terry spies! My mission here is to prevent the invasion of hapless Yudore by the insidious Slox—"

"I hear this!" a rasping, high-pitched voice cut in, from the auxiliary screen, accompanied by a hissing of background noise. A wavering image formed on the tube, steadied into the form of a shiny, purplish-red cranium, long and narrow, knobbed and spiked, with a pair of yellow eyes mounted on outriggers that projected a foot on either side. "I outrage! I do not endure! You are gave one minutes, Eastern Standard

163

Time, for total abandon of vicinity! Counting! Nine, twelve, two, several—"

"Wha—what is it?" Magnan gasped, staring at the newcomer to the conversation.

"Aha—collusion between Soft One and Slox!" Slith keened. "I see it now! You thought to distract my attention with an exchange of civilities whilst your vile cronies executed a sneak attack around left end!"

"I—Chief General Okkyokk—chum to these monstrositaries?" The Slox spokesman screeched. "Such indignant my language lack! Insufficient you threaten to lowly benefits of Slox Protectorate—but addition of insults! My goodness! Drat! Other obscenity as required!"

"It will avail you naught to rant, treacher!" Slith whispered in a venomous tone. "My guns stand ready to answer your slurs!"

"Only incredible restrains of high-class Slox general intrudes herself to spare those skinny neck!" Okkyokk yelled in reply.

"Now, now, gentlemen, don't get carried away," Magnan called over the hiss of static. "I'm sure this can all be worked out equitably—"

"Unless this pernicious meddler in the Groaci destiny disperses his flimsy hulls at once, I'll not be responsible for the result!" Slith declared.

"My frustrate!" Okkyokk yelled, and brandished a pair of anterior limbs tipped with complicated shredding devices. "Gosh, such wish to know sensation of plait all five eyes into single superocular, followed by pluck like obscene daisy!"

"To wait in patience until the happy moment when I officiate at your burial, head-down, in the ceremonial sandbox," Slith countered.

"Well, at least they're still speaking to each other," Magnan said behind his hand as the exchange raged on. "That's something."

"We may get through this without any hull-burns, after all," Retief said. "They have each other bluffed; it looks like talk rather than torpedoes will carry the day. I suggest we execute a strategic withdrawal while they slug it out, vocabulary-to-vocabulary."

"Hmm. Scant points in *that* for Terran diplomacy. That is, duty demands that we play a more creative role in the *rapprochement*." Magnan put a finger against his narrow chin. "Now, if *I* should be the one to propose an equitable solution . . ."

"Let's not remind them we're here, Mr. Magnan," Retief suggested. "Frustrated tempers are often taken out in thrown crockery, and we'd make a convenient teacup—"

"Nonsense, they'd never dare." Magnan leaned forward. "Gentlemen!" he called over the din of battle. "I have the perfect solution! Since there seems to be some lack of confidence on the part of each of you in the benign intentions of the other, I propose that Yudore be placed under a Terran Protectorate!" Magnan smiled expectantly.

There was an instant of total silence as two sets of alien sense organs froze, oriented toward the interruption. Slith was the first to break the paralysis.

"What? Leave the fruits of Groaci planning to Terran harvesting? Never!"

"I convulse!" Okkyokk howled. "I exacerbate! I froth at buccal cavity! How are you invite? Mercy! Heavens to Marmaduke! Et cetera!"

"Gentlemen!" Magnan cried. "We Terrans would only remain on Yudore until such time as the aborigines had been properly educated in modern commercial methods and sexual hygiene, after which we'd withdraw in favor of local self-determination!"

"First to pervert, then to abandon!" Slith hissed. "Bold threats, Soft Ones! But I defy you! General

165

Okkyokk! I propose a truce, whilst we band together to confront the common enemy!"

"Done! Caramba! I effronterize! I mortal insult! I even annoy First destruction we the kibitzer! Then procedure to Slox-Groaci quarrel!"

"Wait!" Magnan yelped. "You don't understand—!"

"I'm afraid they do," Retief said as he reached for the controls. "Hang on for evasive action, Mr. Magnan." The tiny craft leaped ahead, curvetting wildly left and right. There was a flash, and the screens went white and blanked out. The boat bucked wildly and flipped end-for-end. A second detonation sent it spinning like a flat stone skipped over a pond.

"Retief! Stop! We're headed straight for No Man's Land!" Magnan gasped as a lone screen flickered back to life, showing a vast Groaci battle wagon swelling dead ahead.

"We're going in under their guns," Retief snapped. "Running away, we'd be a sitting duck."

"Maybe they'll let us surrender!" Magnan bleated. "Can't we run out a white flag, or something?"

"I'm afraid it would just give them an aiming point." Retief wrenched the boat sideways, rode out another near-miss, drove on, to dive under the big ship's stern.

"Look out!" Magnan screeched as a vast, mottled, blue-green disk slid onto the screen. "We'll crash on Yudore!"

"If we're lucky," Retief agreed. Then the rising scream of splitting air made further conversation impossible.

3

Except for the fading hiss of escaping air and the *ping!* of hot metal contracting, the only sounds audible in the shattered cockpit were Magnan's groans as he extricated himself from the wreckage of his contour chair. Through a rent in the hull, yellow sunlight glared on the smoking ruins of the scout boat's control panel, the twisted and buckled floor plates, the empty pilot's seat.

"Glad to see you're awake," Retief said. Magnan turned his aching head to see his companion leaning in the open escape hatch, apparently intact but for a bruise on the cheekbone and a burned patch on the front of his powder-blue afternoon informal blazer. "The air's a little thin, but the O_2 content seems adequate. How do you feel?"

"Ghastly," Magnan confided. He fumbled his shock harness free and groped his way through the hatch to drop down shakily on a close-cropped, peach-colored sward. All around, tall, treelike growths with ribbed, red-orange trunks rose into the pale sky, supporting masses of spongy, tangerine-toned foliage. Clumps of yellow, amber, and magenta blossoms glowed in the shade like daubs of fluorescent paint.

"Why are we still alive?" the senior diplomat inquired dazedly. "The last thing I remember is a pale-pink mountaintip sticking up through a cloud bank directly in our path."

"We missed it," Retief reassured his chief. "There was just enough power left on our plates to cushion our touchdown. That, and a lot of springy foliage saved our necks."

"Where are we?"

"On a small island in the northen hemisphere, which seems to be the only land on the planet. That's about as specific as I can be, I'm afraid—and I designated the North Pole arbitrarily at that."

"Well—let's get it over with," Magnan sighed, looking around. "Where are they? I suggest we throw ourselves on Slith's mercy. Frankly, I don't trust that

Okkyokk; there's something shifty about those canti-levered oculars of his."

"I'm afraid we won't be able to surrender immediately," Retief said. "Our captors haven't arrived yet."

"Hmm. Doubtless they're making a somewhat less precipitous approach than we. I suppose we might as well make ourselves comfortable."

"On the other hand," Retief said reasonably, "why wait around?"

"What other hope of rescue have we?"

"I don't think either party would make the ideal host—assuming they bother with live prisoners in the first place."

"You're implying that Slith—a fellow bureaucrat—a being with whom I've shared many a convivial cup—would acquiesce in our execution out of hand?" Magnan gasped.

"He might—if he didn't do the job himself first."

"Heavens, Retief, what are we to do? How far do you suppose it is to the nearest native village?"

"I didn't see any signs of civilization on the way down: no towns, no roads or cleared fields. Let's give a listen on the long-wave bands." Retief climbed back inside the wrecked craft, investigated the shock-mounted TRX, spliced a number of broken wires, and twirled the knob. There was nothing but faint static to be heard. He switched to the ship-to-ship frequency.

"—blundering two-eyed imcompetent!" Slith's furious voice came through loud and clear. "Your broken-down excuse for a flagship was closer to them than my own superb standard-bearer! It was your responsibility to blast them from space—"

"My indignant! My furious! Heck! Darn! This accuse from a Five-eyes margarine-fingers! I intolerate! Too bad!"

"Have done!" Slith hissed. "These vituperations

168

avail us naught! If the Soft Ones survive to make known that we fired on a Terran vessel—in self-defense, of course—a horde of their execrable Peace Enforcers will descend on us like bim beetles in grub-harvest time!"

"I proposterate! My laughter! Your numbskull! Alive, oh! After such crashing, entirely! No, unpossible; I rediculate! *Au contraire,* I suggestion my resumption our dispute. Where were? Indeed, yes—my descriptioning your ancestry—"

"Hark, mindless one! Like other low forms of life, the Soft Ones are tenacious of vitality. We must make sure of their demise! Hence, I shall descend to administer the *coup de grâce* to any survivors, whilst you stand by off-planet—or, preferably, withdraw to neutral space—"

"So you enable to theft these planet, unoppositioned? My amuse! My hylerical! Goodness me! I accompanate, quite so!"

"Very well—if you insist. You may accompany me aboard my personal gunboat. I'll designate a modest destroyer escort to convoy us down to the surface."

"Nix. I preference to my own vessel, gratitudes anyhow. And my bring few Slox cruiser in order to not lonesome."

"Cruisers?" Slith said harshly. "In that case, I think a pair of Groaci battleships would be in order—just to balance the formation, you understand."

"Combination operate incompletion unless Slox battlewagon also include!"

"Actually," Slith hissed, "I see no reason not to bring my entire fleet along—just in case you should entertain ideas of a sneak attack during my absence!"

"My agreeness! I, too! The more the merriment! Gracious me! Full speed ahead! Devil take the hind parts!"

"Agreed! Roger and out," Slith snapped.

"Good heavens, Retief," Magnan muttered, "those two madmen are going to stage a full-scale invasion, just to keep an eye on each other—"

"No one could accuse us now of having failed to influence the course of Slox-Groaci relations," Retief said calmly. "Well, let's be off. We have about an hour before they arrive." Quickly, he detached the compact radio from its mountings, extracted an emergency ration pack from the debris.

"Which way?" Magnan queried worriedly, staring at the deep-orange shade of the forest all around.

"Take your choice, Mr. Magnan," Retief said, indicating the four points of the compass. "Eeenie, meenie, miney, or moe."

"Hmm. I think perhaps due meenie; it looks a tiny bit less forbidding; or possibly just a few points to the miney of meenie."

"Meenie by miney it is," Retief said, and led the way into the tall timber.

4

"Retief—I'm utterly exhausted," Magnan panted three quarters of an hour and three miles from the wrecked scout boat.

"We're not clear yet," Retief said. "We'd better keep going, and rest later."

"I'd as soon face a Groaci firing squad as die of heart failure and heat prostration." Magnan sank down on the yielding turf, lay breathing in great gulps.

"How about a Slox skinning party?" Retief suggested. "I understand they start with the scalp and work downward, like peeling a banana."

170

"Jape if you must," Magnan groaned. "I'm past caring." He sat up suddenly, staring suspiciously at a small, bell-shaped blossom, with petals of a delicate shade of coral pink.

"Bees," he said distastefully. "Allergic as I am even to Terran insects, a sting from an alien form would probably be instantly fatal."

"Still, as you pointed out, one demise is pretty much like another." Retief consoled his superior. "If it actually was a bee you saw, it's the first native animal life to make its presence known."

"I didn't see it—but I heard it distinctly," Magnan said severely. "It buzzed practically in my ear."

"This is a rather curious forest," Retief observed. "Only one variety of tree, one kind of grass, one type of flower, in assorted sizes and colors. But no weeds. No parasitic vines. No big trees crowding out smaller ones, no stunted growth. Not even any deadfalls."

"Ummp," Magnan grunted. "Retief, suppose for the nonce we succeed in eluding capture; what then? Nobody knows we're here. How will we ever be rescued?"

"Interesting question, Mr. Magnan."

"Not that it matters a great deal," Magnan went on morosely. "With my mission a failure—worse than a failure—my career is in ruins!" He groaned. "Do you realize that if it hadn't been for our meddling, this invasion would probably never have come to pass?"

"The thought had occurred to me," Retief conceded.

"To say nothing of the loss of the scout boat. If the Undersecretary holds me responsible—holds *us* responsible, I should say—that is, in the event he doesn't hold *you* personally responsible, Retief, as pilot—why, you'll be years paying it off," he went on more cheerfully. "Still, I'll put in a word for you. After all, Slith *was* shooting at us."

"There is that."

"And actually, who's to say it was my friendly attempt to offer a compromise that precipitated the invasion? I daresay the hotheads would have embarked on their conquest in any event."

"Possibly," Retief agreed.

"Actually, by engaging them in conversation, I doubtless delayed the inevitable for a . . . a length of time."

"Several seconds, at least."

"Why, actually, Retief, by offering myself as a sacrifice on the altar of interbeing chumship, I may have saved countless lives!"

"I suppose a certain number of bacteria were lost in our crash landing," Retief pointed out.

"You scoff," Magnan charged. "But history will vindicate my stand! Why, I wouldn't be surprised if a special posthumous medal were struck—" He broke of with a start. "There it is again!" He scrambled up. "It sounded like an enraged hornet! Where did it go?"

Retief cocked his head, listening, then leaned over to examine the clump of apricot-colored flowers nodding on long stems, beside which Magnan had been sitting.

"Don't waste time plucking nosegays!" Magnan yelped. "I'm under attack!"

"Mr. Magnan, I don't think there are any insects in the vicinity," Retief demurred.

"Eh? Why, I can hear them quite plainly!" Magnan frowned. "It sounds like one of those old fashioned hand-crank telephones still in use out on Jawbone, when you leave it off the hook."

"Close, Mr. Magnan," Retief said, and leaned down to put his ear to the trumpet-shaped bloom.

"Well, I thought you'd *never* speak!" a tiny voice said distinctly in his ear.

5

"Buzzing blossoms is quite fantastic enough," Magnan said wonderingly, "but talking tulips! Who'd ever believe it?"

". . . somebody to converse with," the cricket-sized voice was saying. "I'm dying to know all the news. Now, just tell me all about yourself: your hopes, your dreams, how you happened to be here—everything!"

Retief held a blossom to his lips as if it were indeed the mouthpiece of a phone. "I'm Retief; this is my colleague, Mr. Magnan. Whom have we the honor of addressing?"

"Well, nice to know you, Retief. And Mister Magnan, too. May I call you 'Mister' for short? First names are so much more sort of informal. I'm Herby. Just a nickname, of course. Actually, I don't have a name. At least I didn't have, until dear Renfrew came along. You have no idea what a sheltered life I'd led up until then. Why, do you know, I had the idea I was the only sentient intelligence in the Galaxy?"

"Who . . . who are you?" Magnan blurted. *"Where* are you? Why is the microphone camouflaged to look like a plant?"

"Camouflage? Why, there's no camouflage, mister. You see me just as I am."

"But—I don't see you at all!" Magnan complained, looking around warily. "Where are you hiding?"

"You're squeezing me at this very moment," Herby said.

"You mean—" Magnan held the faintly aromatic blossom at arm's length and stared at it. "You mean —I'm . . . you're . . . we're . . ."

"Now you're getting the idea," the voice said encouragingly.

"Talking flowers—here, in the middle of nowhere —and speaking Terran at that? I must be hallucinating! I've been driven mad by hardship!"

"I doubt it, Mr. Magnan," Retief said soothingly. "I hear it too."

"If I can imagine I hear voices coming out of posies, I can imagine you hearing them too," Magnan retorted tartly.

"Oh, I'm real enough," the voice said reassuringly. "Why should you doubt me?"

"Who taught you to speak Terran?" Retief asked.

"Renfrew. I learned so much from him. Curious— but before he came, it never occurred to me to be lonely—"

"Who is Renfrew?"

"A friend. A very dear friend."

"Retief, this is fantastic!" Magnan whispered. "Are there . . . are there many like you?" he inquired of the bloom.

"No—just me. After all, there'd hardly be room, you know—"

"What a coincidence!" Magnan exclaimed. "One talking plant on the entire world, and we stumble on it in the first hour! I'm beginning to think our luck is still holding!"

"Now, where are you from, if you don't mind my asking?" the plant inquired.

"We're Terrans," Magnan said. "And I'm sure we're going to get on famously, er, Herby."

"But—I understood Terra was the name of Renfrew's home planet . . . ?"

"Quite so. Marvelous place, you'd love it, now that all the jungles have been cleared and replaced by parking lots . . ." Magnan caught himself. "Ah, no

174

offense intended, of course," he added hastily. "Why, some of my best friends are plants."

"Heavens—all three of you from one planet? No wonder you left! Such overcrowding "

"Yes—now, Mr. Herby—if you could just tell us the way to the nearest native settlement . . ."

"Buildings, you mean, and streets, spaceports, that sort of thing?"

"Yes! Preferably not one of these dismal provincial towns. Something in a modest metropolis will do—"

"Sorry, there isn't one—though Renfrew told me about them, of course."

Magnan groaned. "No towns at all? Then . . ."

"Just jungle."

"If this fellow Renfrew has a ship, we may be able to catch a ride with him. I wonder—could we meet him . . . ?"

"Well—I suppose so, mister. He's quite nearby, as it happens—"

"He's still here, then?"

"Oh, yes indeed."

"Saved," Magnan breathed in relief. "Can you direct us, Herby?"

"Certainly. Just press on meenie, bearing a little to the miney after you cross the stream, then hard moe at the lake. You can't miss him."

Magnan looked startled. "How did you know?" He frowned at Retief in puzzlement. "I thought *we* named the local directions . . ."

"Oh, indeed," Herby spoke up. "I merely employed your own nomenclature."

"You must have a fantastic ear," Magnan said wonderingly. "That discussion was held miles from here."

"I don't miss much," Herby said complacently.

"He's remarkably sophisticated for such a modest bloom," Magnan commented as they started off.

"I suspect most of Herby is underground, Mr. Mag-

175

nan," Retief pointed out. "There's no room for a speech center in the part we saw."

"Gad—a subterranean cerebrum—like a giant potato?" Magnan said uneasily, treading lightly. "A spooky thought, Retief."

Twenty minutes' brisk hike brought the two Terrans to the shore of a small, gurgling brook overhung with majestically arching foliage. They followed the bank to the right for a quarter of a mile, at which point the waters spilled down in a foaming amber cataract into a placid pond half a mile across.

"So far so good," Magnan said uncertainly. "But I see no signs of habitation, not even a hut, to say nothing of a ship . . ."

Retief moved past Magnan toward a dense thicket which obtruded somewhat from the smooth line of trees edging the lakeshore. He parted the broad, copper-colored leaves, revealing a surface of rust-pitted metal curving away into the dimness.

"Lousy Ann II"—he read the corroded letters welded to the crumbling hull plates. "Looks like we've found Renfrew's ship." He pulled a low-growing branch aside. "And here's Renfrew."

"Splendid! Magnan hurried up, halted abruptly to stare in horror at the heap of moldering bones topped by a grinning skull still wearing a jaunty yachting cap.

"That's . . . Renfrew?" he quavered.

"Quite so," said a deep voice from somewhere overhead. "And take my word for it, mister—it's been a long, lonely time since he sat down there."

6

"Two hundred years, give or take a decade or two," Retief said as he climbed out through the derelict's sagging port, brushing the dust and rust-scale from his hands. "She was a Concordiat-registered racing sloop, converted for long-range cruising. What's left of the crew quarters suggests she was fitted out for one-man operation."

"That's right," agreed the resonant baritone—which, the Terrans had determined, emanated from a large, orchidlike blossom sprouting amid the foliage twenty feet above their heads. "Just Renfrew. It was a small world he inhabited, but he seemed content with it. Not that he was stand-offish, of course. He was as friendly as could be—right up until the difficulty about his leaving."

"What sort of, ah, difficulty?" Magnan inquired.

"He seemed quite upset that his vessel was unable to function. I did my best to console him; regaled him with stories and poems, sang merry songs—"

"Where did you learn them?" Magnan cut in sharply. "I understood Renfrew was the first Terran to visit here."

"Why, from him, of course."

"Good lord—imagine having your own chestnuts endlessly repeated back at you," Magnan whispered behind his hand.

"Did you ever tell a joke to an Ambassador?" Retief inquired.

"A telling point," Magnan conceded. "But at least they usually add a little variety by garbling the punch line."

"How did Renfrew happen to crash-land here?" Retief inquired.

"Oh, he didn't; he came to rest very gently."

"Then, why couldn't he take off again?" Magnan demanded.

"I believe he described it as foreign matter in the warpilator field windings," the voice replied vaguely. "But let's not talk about the past. The present is so much more exciting! Heavens! There hasn't been such activity here since the last glacial age!"

"Retief—there's something slightly piscine about this situation," Magnan murmured. "I'm not sure I trust these garrulous gardenias. Herby said he was the only one of his kind on the planet—yet here's another equally verbose vegetable."

"Oh, that was quite true," the voice above spoke up promptly. "Why in the world would I lie to you?"

"Kindly refrain from eavesdropping," Magnan said coldly. "This happens to be a personal conversation."

"Not as personal as calling me a potato-brain," the orchid said a trifle coolly.

"Goodness—I hope you don't listen to irresponsible gossip," Magnan replied with dignity. "Do I appear the type to employ such an epithet?" He put his mouth to Retief's ear. "The grapevine here surpasses anything I've encountered, even at a diplomatic reception!"

"Now, let me see:" the voice from on high mused. "You mentioned something called a parking lot. I'd like to know more about that, and—"

"I suppose Herby told you that, too!" Magnan snapped. "If I'd known he was such a blabbermouth, I'd never have confided in him! Come, Retief—we'll withdraw to where we can have a modicum of privacy."

"As to that, Mr. Magnan—" Retief started.

"Not here," Magnan interrupted. He led the way a

hundred feet down the shore, halted under a spreading bough. "It's apparent I was indiscreet with that Herby person," he said from the corner of his mouth, without moving his lips. "I see now he was a rumormonger of the worst stripe, in addition to being of questionable veracity. Sole representative of his race, indeed! Why, I suspect every shrub in sight has a wagging tongue!"

"Very probably," Retief agreed.

"There's nothing to do now, quite obviously," Magnan said, "but select an honest-looking plant and approach the problem afresh, impressing the vegetable with our sincerity and benign intentions. Then, when we've wormed our way into its confidence, we can determine how to make use of it to our own best advantage. How does it sound?"

"Familiar," Retief said.

"Excuse me . . ." Magnan jumped a foot as a voice squeaked the words almost in his ear. "What does 'sincerity' mean in this context?"

"Very little," Retief addressed a cluster of small, russet buds almost invisible among the roan leaves overhead.

"Is there no privacy to be found anywhere in the confounded wilderness?" Magnan inquired with asperity.

"I'm afraid not," the miniature voice piped. "As I was telling you a while ago, there's not a great deal I miss."

"A while ago?" Magnan repeated with a rising inflection. "Why, we've only just met!"

"I don't understand, mister. I'm Herby. You know me!"

"Nonsense! Herby is a little chap growing under a tree a mile from here."

"Of course! I grow everywhere, naturally. After all, it's my island, isn't it? Not that I'm not willing to share it with a few friends."

"Utter nonsense!" Magnan sputtered. "I might have known a potato was incapable of coherent thought!"

"Herby's telling the truth," Retief said. "It's all one plant: the trees, the grass—everything. Like a banyan tree, only more so." He examined a flower closely. "There's a tympanic membrane that serves as both microphone and speaker. Very ingenious of Mother Nature."

"In that case—they—or it—"

"He," Retief amended.

"He's overheard every word that's been spoken since we landed." Magnan addressed the blossoms directly: "Look here, Herby—you're aware that we're distressed diplomats, marooned here by an unfortunate accident—"

"I thought Slith and that other fellow—Okkyokk—were responsible," Herby corrected. "They seem dreadfully argumentative chaps. I do wish they'd lower their voices."

"Quite. Now, you're aware of their hostile intentions toward Mr. Retief and myself—"

"Oh, my," Herby interrupted, "they *do* seem upset. Such language!"

"Yes. Now, as I was saying . . ." Magnan paused. "What do you mean, 'such language'?"

"I was referring to Grand Commander Slith's rather graphic use of invective," Herby explained. "Not that General Okkyokk isn't holding his own, of course. I must say my vocabulary is expanding rapidly!"

"You speak as though you could hear them now," Magnan commented, puzzled.

"Ummm. On the ship-to-shore band."

"But—you don't have a radio—do you?"

"A what?"

"If he has organs for detecting sound," Retief said, "why not organs for picking up short wave?"

"Why—that's remarkable!" Magnan exclaimed.

"But short wave? It would be rather too much to hope that you can *send* as well as receive . . . ?"

"Why, I suppose I *could* transmit, via my snarf-nodes, if there were any reason to."

"Retief—we're saved!" Magnan caroled. "Herby—send the following message at once: Ah . . . Special Priority-Z Mayday, CDT Sector HQ, Aldo Cerise. CDT 87903 subject unprovoked attack—no, make that unwarranted attack—resulting in emergency planetfall—"

"Oh, I'm sorry, mister," Herby cut in. "I couldn't send that."

"But—why not?"

"Why, if I did, some nose parker might come and take you away."

"I sincerely hope so!"

"I've waited two hundred standard years for someone to talk to," Herby said in a hurt tone. "Now you're talking of rushing off. Well, I won't do it."

"The SOS is our sole hope!" Magnan cried. "Would you stand in the way of our rescue?"

"Please—calm yourself, mister. Look at Retief: *he's* not making a scene. Just resign yourself to the fact that you'll spend the rest of your life here, and we'll get on famously—just as Renfrew and I did—right up until the last few days."

"The rest of our lives?" Magnan gasped. "But—but that's unthinkable! We may linger on for another fifty years!"

"Not if Slith has his way," Retief said. "Where are they now, Herby?"

"I was about to say," Herby began, "they would be arriving any moment . . ." The vegetable voice was drowned by a rising drone that swelled swiftly to a bellowing roar. A sleek, shark-nosed shape swept overhead, followed by another, two more, then an entire squadron. Sonic booms crashed across the jungle, laying patterns of shock ripples across the still water of the lake. Treetops whipped in the turbulent wakes as two battle fleets hurtled past at low altitude, dwindled, were gone.

"You see?" Herby said a trifle breathlessly into the echoing silence. "Two's company, but a crowd is altogether too much!"

Retief twisted the knob of the radio slung at his belt.

". . . pinpointed our quarry!" Slith's breathy voice was keening. "If you will employ your units in enrircling the south shore of the island, General, I shall close the pincer to the north."

"Looks like they've spotted us," Retief said. "Slith must carry better optical and IR gear than I gave him credit for."

Sunlight winked on distant craft circling back to spread out on the far side of the lake, sinking down out of sight behind the massed foliage of the forest. Other vessels were visible to left and right, and behind them.

"Not much point in running cross-country," Retief said thoughtfully. "They've got us surrounded."

"What are we going to do?" Magnan yelped. "We can't just stand here!"

"Ouch!" Herby said suddenly. "Ooh! Ahh!"

"What's the matter?" Magnan leaped in alarm, staring around him.

"Why, that hurts like anything!" Herby exclaimed indignantly.

"It's the landing blasts." Retief indicated the smoke rising from points all around the compass. "The Groaci still use old-style reaction motors for atmospheric maneuvering. Must be scorching Herby quite painfully."

Magnan gasped. "You see what sort of uncouth ruffians they are?" he said indignantly. "Now, wouldn't you like to change your mind, Herby, and assist us—"

"And collect a new crop of third-degree burns when your friends arrive? No, thank you! It's out of the question!"

"A deep-toned whickering sound had started up, grew quickly louder.

"A heli," Retief said. "They're not wasting any time."

In the shelter of the tree the two Terrans watched the approach of the small, speedy craft. It swung out over the lake, riffling the water, and hovered two hundred feet in the air.

"ATTENTION, TERRY SPIES!" an electronically amplified voice boomed out from it. "SURRENDER AT ONCE OR SUFFER A FATE UNSPEAKABLE!"

"Herby—if those barbarians get their hands on us, our usefulness as conversationalists will come to an abrupt end," Magnan said urgently.

"YOU HAVE BEEN WARNED!" the PA blared. "EMERGE AT ONCE, EMPTY-HANDED!"

"Maybe we can hide out in this dense growth," Magnan said, "if Herby will keep us apprised of their whereabouts. Maybe we can elude capture until help comes."

The copter had drifted closer.

"THIRTY SECONDS," the big voice boomed. "IF AT THE END OF THAT TIME YOU HAVE NOT SUBMITTED YOURSELVES TO GROACI JUSTICE, THE ENTIRE ISLAND WILL BE ENGULFED IN FIRE!"

"Cook us alive?" Magnan gasped. "They wouldn't!"

"Retief . . . mister . . ." Herby said worriedly. "Did he mean?"

"I'm afraid so, Herby," Retief said. "But don't worry. We won't let matters proceed that far. Shall we go, Mr. Magnan?"

Magnan swallowed with difficulty. "I suppose a comfortable garroting in a civilized cell *is* preferable to broiling alive," he said in a choked voice as they walked out from the shade into the bright-orange sunlight of the beach.

7

"A wise decision, Soft Ones," Slith whispered. "In return for your cooperation, I give my reassurances that your remains will be transmitted to your loved ones suitably packaged, with a friendly note explaining that you fell foul of the alert Groacian antispy apparatus and were dispatched ere my personal intervention could save you from the just retribution your crimes deserved."

"Why, that's very thoughtful of you, I'm sure, Grand Commander," Magnan said, mustering a ghastly smile. "But might I suggest just one teensy change? Why not intervene just a bit sooner, and return us safe and sound—a stirring gesture of interbeing amity—"

"My researches into the Terry nature," Slith interrupted, steepling his eyes—an effect which failed to reassure his listeners—"indicate that your kith respond most generously to those who adhere to a policy of unanswering hostility. This evidence of Groaci determination will evoke, I doubt not, a sizable increase in the Terry subsidy to the Keep Groac Gray drive— funds which will of course be quietly diverted to our urgently needed naval modernization program, by the way."

"But why?" Magnan clanked his chains disconsolately. "Why can't we all just be dear, dear friends?"

"Alas," Slith said. "Aside from the fact that we Groaci find you Soft Ones singularly repellent to all

184

nine senses, rendering social intercourse awkward, and the further fact that Terran ambitions Galactic-expansionwise conflict with manifest Groaci destiny—plus the fact that I owe you suitable recompense for your malicious sabotage of my mercantile efforts at Haunch II—aside from these matters, I say—it's necessary at this juncture to silence you."

"S-silence us?" Magnan said. "Why, heavens, Commander Slith—if you're referring to the little misunderstanding that led to our unscheduled landing here on Yudore, don't give it a thought! Why, I've already forgotten it! Actually, it was probably just pilot error on the part of my colleague, Mr. Retief—"

"He's not talking about that, Mr. Magnan," Retief said. "He's talking about his use of Yudore as a red herring to cover an attack on the Slox Empire."

"Silence, verbose one!" Slith hissed; but Okkyokk, whose image on the conference screen had been quietly occupying a complicated perch in the background, spoke up:

"Who this? My fasinate! Gosh! Tell more!"

"Fool!" Slith leaped to his feet, vibrating his throat sac at Retief. "Your groundless insinuations deprive you of life's last sweet moments!" He signaled the guards. "On with the executions, forthwith!"

"Not so hurry, Five-eyes!" Okkyokk snarled. "Conversation me, Terry; my interest, oh yes! Tell on!"

"Keep out of this, Okkyokk!" Slith hissed as the guards started forward eagerly.

"My listen!" Okkyokk yelled. "Your forgot, Slith—I guns train on you! My chat these Terry—blow your in fragmentation, or!"

"Better humor him, Slith," Retief said. "Inasmuch as your feet consists of disguised barges with dummy guns, you're in no position to call his bluff."

Slith made spluttering sounds.

"No gun?" Okkyokk chortled. "Good new tonight! Tell more, Terry!"

"It's quite simple," Retief lured you out here to get your gunboats out of the way so he could proceed to attack the Slox home planets with minimal interference. The bombardment is probably underway right now."

"Lies!" Slith found his frail voice. "Okkyokk—heed not the treacher's vile fables! He seeks to set us at odds, each with other!"

"I grateful you extreme, Terry!" the Slox Commander grated in a voice like a steel girder shearing, ignoring Slith's appeal. "Preparation you for dead, Groaci bigshot! Fake up big war, eh, you tell. Make fool allbody, eh? Then join force and invasion Terries, eh? Fruits and nuts! You never delusion me for every! Hold on hats, kids—"

"Don't fire!" Slith screeched. "The Soft One lies— which I can prove in most dramatic fashion—by blasting your cancerous aggregation of derelicts into their component atoms!"

"Retief—say something!" Magnan yelped. "If they start shooting—"

"Then you Soft Ones will die!" Slith hissed. "If *they* prevail—you die with my flagship—and if I prevail— then long shall you linger under the knives of my virtuosi!"

"How you plan do so big shoot with empty gun?" Okkyokk inquired warily.

"Retief!" Slith cried. "Confess to him you lied—else will I decree torments yet uninvented to adorn your passing!"

"Better open fire quick—if you can," Retief said. "As for you, General," he adressed the screen, "it always pays to get in the first lick—"

"Retief, what are you saying?" Magnan yelped.

186

"Why goad them to this madness? No matter who wins, we lose!"

"My confuse!" Okkyokk stated. "Splendor idea, shoot up unarmed Five-eyes—but what if Terry big lying?"

"Don't let him get the jump on you, Slith," Retief advised.

"Gunnery Officer!" the Groaci Commander hissed in sudden agonized decision. "All batteries—open salvo fire!"

The response was instanteous; a series of hollow clicking sounds over the intercom. Then the dumbfounded voice of the Gunnery Officer:

"Exalted one—I regret to report . . ."

"Sabotage!" Slith yelled. On the screen, Okkyokk paused, one digital member poised above a large puce button.

"How, no explosing? Gun fails operationing, just as Terry inform? Splendor!" the Slox leader waggled his ocular extrusions. "Now time procedure to extermination you with leisurely! Master Gunner—procedure blow picture window in Five-eyes flagship, give Commander Slith good viewing of eventuals!"

Slith hissed and sprang for the door, where he fought for position with the guards who had reached the portal before him. Magnan covered his ears and screwed his eyes shut.

"Whats?" Okkyokk's puzzled voice was coming from the screen. "Hows? Malfunctionate of firepower at times like these? My intolerate! Caramba! Oh, heck!"

"I suggest both you gentlemen relax," Retief raised his voice slightly over the hubbub. "No one's going to do any shooting."

"So . . . your spies have infiltrated my flagship!" Slith hissed. "Little will it avail you, Retief! Once in space, my most creative efforts will be lavished on

187

your quivering corpori!" He scrabbled on the rug, came up with his command mike. "Engineer! Lift off, emergency crash procedures!"

"Another disappointment in store, I'm afraid, Slith," Retief said as no surge of acceleration followed. "Herby's particularly sensitive to rocket blasts," he explained gently. "Ergo—no gunfire."

"Herby?" Slith keened, waggling his eyes, from which the jeweled shields had fallen in the tussle. "Herby?"

"Herby," Okkyokk muttered. "What Herby, which?"

"Herby!" Magnan gasped. "But . . . but . . ."

"Undone?" Slith whispered. "Trapped here by the treachery of the insidious Soft Ones? But briefly shall you gloat, my Retief!" The Groaci jerked the elaborately ornamented power-gun from the plastic alligator-hide holster at his bony hip, took aim . . .

"Three and out," Retief said, as Slith stared in goggle-eyed paralysis at the small, coral-toned flower growing from the barrel of the weapon. "Herby appreciates my conversation far too much to let you blow holes in me. Right, Herby?"

"Quite so, Retief," a cricket-sized voice chirped from the dainty blossom.

"My departure, golly whiz!" Okkyokk's voice blasted from the screen. "Navigationer—full fast ahead!"

"No use, General," Retief said. "Everybody's grounded. Your field windings are full of vines, I'm afraid."

"So that's why Renfrew couldn't leave!" Magnan gulped. "I knew it all along, of course."

"What does this mean?" Slith whispered.

"It means you've been conquered single-handed by a population of one," Retief addressed the alien leaders. "So—if you're ready, gentlemen, I'm sure Herby will be willing to discuss the terms of your surrender."

8

"Heavens, Retief," Magnan said, adjusting the overlapping puce lapels of his top-formal midmorning cutaway in the gilt-framed mirror outside the impressive mahogany doors of the Undersecretary for Extraterrestrial Affairs. "If we hadn't seized a moment to transmit a distress call on Slith's TX while Herby was busy taking the surrender, we might still be languishing in boredom on that dismal island."

"I doubt if we'd have been bored," Retief pointed out, "with several hundred grounded sailors roaming the woods blaming us for their troubles."

"What a ghastly experience, with every bush and bough jabbering away in coloquial Slox and accentless Groaci, carrying on twelve hundred scrambled conversations at once!"

"In time I think Herby would have mastered the knack of segregating his dialogues," Retief said. "Even with a slice missing from that four-mile-long brain the soundings showed, he should be a fast learner."

"He certainly mastered the technique of creative negotiation with record speed," Magnan agreed. "I can't help feeling a trifle sorry for poor Slith and Okkyokk; their fleets consigned to molder on the ground, the while they supply teams of conversationalists in relays in perpetuity for the diversion of their conqueror."

Retief and Magnan turned as the elevator doors opened behind them. An orderly emerged, pushing a teacart on which rested a handsome teak tub containing a tall, lilylike plant topped by a six-inch flower, glowing a healthy pink and yellow.

"Ah, gentlemen," the blossom greeted them in a mellow tenor voice, "I'm happy to report that new scenes seem to stimulate me—or at least this slice of me!"

Magnan shuddered delicately. "Imagine sprouting a bureaucrat from a wedge of frontal lobe," he said behind his hand. "It makes my head ache just to think of it."

A slender man with thick spectacles thrust his head from the Secretarial suite.

"The Secretary will see you now," he announced, and held the door as the orderly wheeled the cart through.

"Mr. Secretary," Magnan said grandly, "I have the honor to present His Excellency the Herbaceous Ambassador."

"Delighted to meet you, sir or madam," Thunderstroke rumbled inclining his head graciously to the bloom, which nodded in reply. "Now—do tell me all the details of how you captured two fully armed war fleets . . ."

Retief and Magnan withdrew, leaving the Undersecreatry listening attentively to his visitor's account of the sapless victory.

"Lobotomy seems to agree with Herby," Magnan observed complacently. "Well, I must hurry along, Retief. I have a modest cutting I plan to infiltrate into the flowerbed under the Groaci Ambassador's window." He hurried off.

"Tsk," said a tiny voice from the pink boutonniere adorning Retief's topmost lapel. "The segment of me you left with the Undersecretary is being regaled with a rather gamey anecdote about cross-fertilizing tearose begonias . . ."

"It's not considered polite to listen in on private conversations, Herby," Retief pointed out.

"How can I help it?" the blossom protested. "After all, it's me he's talking to!"

"Just don't repeat what you hear. Unless," Retief added as he strolled off toward the Chancery bar, "it's something you think I really ought to know . . ."

168